CHASE

The $ecret Billionaire $ociety

BOOK 1

NANCY PENNICK

Allison-Hayes Publishing

ISBN-10: 1-7347996-0-9
ISBN-13: 978-1-7347996-0-6

The Secret Billionaire Society series is dedicated to my family who have loved, helped and supported me through this process.

PROLOGUE

"Mr. Chase Young?" a voice said over the speakers.

"Yes." I held up my hand, feeling like I was back in grade school and the teacher was taking attendance. I inhaled and slowly let it out. We were six stupid sons of bitches. What were we thinking? But, here we were, too late now.

The man behind the mirror. We'd never met him. We didn't know what he looked like. Yet, we'd agreed to put our lives in his hands and trust him.

We only knew his name—Mr. Smith. He was now in charge of us, the Secret Billionaire Society, which started as a joke in college. Funny, but if truth be told, each of us made the Forbes Top100 list at one time or another in the past decade.

We'd known each other since college, a collection of guys from all parts of the country who immediately clicked. Since then, we had been a tight group, celebrating our birthdays on one chosen day each year. No matter where we were or what we'd been doing, we dropped everything and showed up at the designated time and place.

We had hired Mr. Smith, sight unseen, during a drunken thirtieth birthday party. Someone, no make that all of us, had an epiphany at the end of the night. The time had come to drop our partying ways, get off page six and start contributing to society. Heard it before? So had we. Perhaps the alcohol consumed during the night muddled our brains, but we thought we had the answer to world peace by the time we finished.

To some extent, we were familiar faces to the public and did not want to be recognized, especially if we failed. We needed to blend into the general population. The idea of a middleman came to the six of us during the last toast of the evening. We joked it could be like *Mission Impossible*. The movie team never saw or knew the person who gave their assignments. Then boom! It was like lightning had struck us. We laughed, slapped each other on the back and the idea was born. We needed a guy similar to *Mission Impossible* to help us achieve world peace.

Beau, the most tech savvy of us, dove into his computer, searching for help. He made a few phone calls, put the last one on speaker, and we interviewed the man or woman on the spot. Yeah, he had a man's voice, but could have used a device to disguise it. Maybe Mr. Smith didn't want us to know who he was either.

After many hours of discussion, the billionaires were satisfied with his answers and told Mr. Smith he was hired. Funny thing, he didn't want to be paid. He said he had his own altruistic motives and liked our idea. He wanted to be part of the team. *But.* There was always a but in negotiations, right? Something had to be at stake, otherwise we could easily back out. Fine, we said, and agreed to his terms. Mr. Smith would receive all we owned if we did not follow through with the assignments. Maybe he didn't have selfless goals after all, but we didn't want to quit. We wouldn't give up and knew we could accomplish anything we set our minds to. Hell, at five in the morning nothing sounded impossible.

We were instructed to put together dossiers. A special phone would be sent to each of us and when the flash drives were loaded and ready, we were to type a code into the cell. Once sent, a date and time came back with a password to use with the courier. He'd come to our house to pick up the memory stick and deliver it to Mr. Smith. The phone would then self-destruct. He'd thought of everything.

Once the documents were in Smith's hands, he'd know everything about us. The only thing we asked was to give us separate assignments. After receiving and reading our bios, instructions would be sent by a delivery person. Mr. Smith took no chances and didn't want us to use our cell phones, email, texts, or any technical means of communication. Eventually, we'd have private phones to contact him.

We'd now been summoned into what I can only describe as an interrogation room, as seen on TV, to wait for Mr. Smith. In all the shows, the cops and detectives stood on one side watching through a one-way mirror, while the perp was questioned on the other. The room had been requested by our mentor, and he would not start the missions until construction was complete.

A trusted contractor built the place, a two-room soundproof dwelling, on my property. Mr. Smith could slip into a special entrance directly connected to the darkened side of the one-way mirror room without being seen. The outer waiting room was the typical man cave with a huge TV screen mounted on one wall. Loungers, a bar with comfort food, and the latest tech gear filled the rest of the room.

When we got word Mr. Smith had arrived in a limo with darkened windows, we began to fidget in our seats. Shit. What had we gotten into? But we'd all signed a binding contract. Our assets had been put in a trust, and we wouldn't get our fortunes back until all six of us completed our assignments. I scratched the side of my jaw, a nervous habit which gave away what I was thinking, my tell, making me very bad at poker. A bead of sweat trickled down the side of my head, and I swiped at it, chastising myself. I had nothing to fear. I could do this.

Someone cleared their throat. I stared at my buddies, wondering which one did it. We had the habit of taking things too far, and I waited for another to clear his throat. Nothing happened. Instead, nervous energy flowed through the room, and I was struck by the seriousness of my friends. Here we sat, my five buddies and me, waiting for instructions from the man behind the mirror.

"Mr. Young?" the voice called to me again.

CHAPTER ONE

Grace Edison sat behind her desk at Falcon Airlines shuffling the papers in front of her. She didn't want to look at last month's numbers which had been consistently falling since the beginning of the year. Her father built the airline, and damn her brothers, she was determined it would still succeed. They could care less if they inherited the airline or took it over one day after their dad worked hard to achieve his dream. Her older siblings flew for Falcon but knew they could get jobs anywhere, anytime at more pay.

Someone cleared their throat at her open doorway, startling Grace. She fought for composure and looked away from her computer to see who'd come for a visit. *The banker?* He may be here to call in their loan. *Breathe and smile. A flight attendant?* She tried to solve their problems as quickly as possible and gave competitive pay, yet once a month someone seemed to find a better job. *Game face.*

"Oh." Grace studied the man leaning against the doorway. She looked into his smoldering dark eyes, and if he used them the right way, they would cause her to slip right out of her clothes. He had brunette hair, carefully styled, short on the sides, swept back to one side on top. The close-trimmed beard caused her to internally shudder. Grace loved a man with a beard.

She stood and said, "What can I do to help you?"

The man walking toward her was an inch or two over six feet, causing her to tilt her head. "Hello," he said in a charming voice and extended his hand in greeting. "My name is Chase … Garrett. I'm one of your new pilots."

Grace shook her head. "No, I'm afraid not. We didn't hire any new pilots."

"This *is* Falcon Airlines, if I'm not mistaken. I was told to meet with Grace Edison, Vice President of Operations." Chase slipped his phone from his pocket, flipped through a few screens and produced an email signed by her father, Paul Edison.

Grace bit into her bottom lip as she studied the screen. "Must be some kind of mistake." She didn't want to make eye contact again, throw away all common sense and hire him on the spot.

"Is he here?"

"Who?"

Chase lightly brushed her hand as he took his phone back causing a chill down her spine. "Paul Edison." He pointed over his shoulder. "From the sign on the door, you're Grace Edison, either his daughter or daughter-in-law."

"Daughter."

"If that's your job position, he trusts you."

"Are you questioning why I have the job, Mr. Garrett? Because I'm a woman or his daughter or both?" Grace felt a fire in her belly. Why did she always have to defend the right to her job?

"No, because you are so young." Chase lifted his eyes, connecting to hers.

Grace thought she saw an apology in them somewhere, and the look made her stomach flip. "It's fine. Happens all the time." She clamped her mouth closed. *Why did I say that? Too much information. I am not daddy's little girl who couldn't get a job. I have a business degree! Now he won't take me seriously.*

"Do I report to you for assignments?"

"What did you not understand, Mr. Garrett? You are not a pilot for Falcon Airlines. We did not hire you."

"Please, call me Chase."

Paul Edison, looking fit and tan, popped his head in the door. "Grace? You've met our new pilot, Chase Garrett?" He gestured to Chase.

"Dad, may I speak with you … alone?"

"I'll wait there." Chase cocked his head toward the outer waiting area and left.

"What were you thinking, Dad?" Grace ran her hand through her hair, pushing a blonde lock from her face. "We don't have the money to hire another pilot."

"How are we ever going to expand and grow, Dumpling?"

"Dad!"

"Fine, I forgot. No dumpling comments at work." Paul smiled, and Grace's heart melted. He looked younger than his fifty-eight years, and despite her mom asking for a divorce three years ago, her dad maintained a good outlook on life.

"You work out today?"

"Before I came … heh! You're changing the subject." Paul lifted a forefinger and shook it at her, laughing. "You were always good at that. I thought it was supposed to be the other way around. Parents distract children when they're naughty."

"And you were naughty, Dad! You should have asked me first before you hired a pilot."

"We need one more pilot, Gracie. We're starting the Miami route this week." Paul sank into the chair in front of Grace's desk. "Sit, please. Let's discuss."

"Coffee?" Grace didn't feel like sitting. Her hands were shaking, and she was torn between letting her dad have his way or making a stand. But, if she gave in, she'd have to suffer every day looking at Chase Garrett's handsome face.

"It wouldn't be so bad."

"What wouldn't be so bad?"

Did I say that aloud? "Hiring one more pilot." Grace handed him a mug of steaming black coffee. "But, that's it."

"I promise." Paul leaned back in the chair, sipped his coffee and placed it on the desk. "You know when I started this company, I only had two planes. The administrators at Charlotte Douglas scoffed at me and said I'd never get one of their gates. So, I flew out of Wilgrove Air Park when you were eight years old. Ten years later, I had them eating their words. My little start-up airline, as they called it, had a following. I carved out a specific market and catered to a certain group of people. Low costs, on time and friendly service. I added more cities along the east coast each year. *They* offered me a section of one terminal."

"I know, Dad, I was there."

"Then I don't need to remind you how important this is to me. Investors like to see a profit, Grace. We haven't given them one this year, and I don't understand why."

"You finally said something I can agree on, Dad. I've gone over and over these numbers, and they don't make sense."

"Chase Garrett comes with superb credentials, and he's a handsome guy. Maybe we should use him in our ads. It might help the bottom line."

"Oh, so we're back to him again." Grace refrained from rolling her eyes. She managed to give her dad a humorous smirk. "I thought I told you he was hired."

"Just making sure, darlin'." Paul stood and stretched. "I want Chase to fly the new Miami route.

Orlando and Tampa have been good to us. I want to make a good impression on the execs at Dade."

"On your way out, send him in. I'll give him instructions then send him to personnel to fill out the forms." Grace looked at her dad who grinned from ear to ear. "What?"

"He's good-looking, right?" Paul nodded his head. "Be open to new possibilities, Dumpling."

Grace searched for something harmless she could throw, but Paul slipped through the door before she got a chance. She sat back in her seat with a huff and spun away from the door. Tears had filled her eyes, and she needed to gain her composure before Chase returned. "Open to new possibilities?" she mumbled. "I don't know if it will ever be my reality."

"Ms. Edison?" His voice sounded close.

What is he, a cat? I didn't hear him come in! Grace pulled a tissue from its box on the table behind her desk. "I got something in my eye. Give me a minute." She dabbed quickly and hoped her eyelashes didn't leave mascara traces on her cheeks.

"And, please call me Grace." Grace turned in her chair and found Chase standing with one hand folded over the other right in front of her desk. "I want to apologize, Chase. My dad and I had a miscommunication. You're hired. Can you start tomorrow?" She lifted a shoulder. "You won't be in the air or called upon for duty. I want you to meet my brothers and go over the basics. They're pilots and in charge of scheduling, maintenance, flight patterns and the like. Your resume says you have a commercial pilot's license. Bring it with you tomorrow. Our jet pilots start at 90K. Hope it's all right with you."

Chase nodded to everything she said. *Strange, he seems too eager.* She had low-balled the starting salary but the expression on his face never changed. He wasn't insulted by the offer. Grace put the thought out of her head but planned to get back to it later. "Any questions before I send you to personnel?"

"What time tomorrow?" Chase smiled, showing straight white teeth.

Grace flipped open the airline schedule on her computer and scrolled through it. "Tim and Mark should be here at eight a.m. If you come at eight-thirty, I can talk with them first."

* * * *

Chase hoped he appeared agreeable to everything she said. He'd followed orders and couldn't wait to call Mr. Smith. Grace's reaction to his hire meant Falcon Airlines must have financial problems. The solution seemed like a quick fix. He would personally invest money into the company if it would help them stay afloat. His assignment would be over, and his good deed was done. He could go home to his house in Myers Park, an easy drive away. He didn't understand why he had to stay in a crappy apartment near the city in the first place. "Mr. Smith is the boss," he mumbled to himself.

When he arrived at his parking spot, Chase pounded the roof of the five-year-old Honda Accord he'd been given to drive and unlocked the door. Before sliding behind the wheel, Chase took one look back at Falcon Headquarters. The eye of the bird glared at him from the middle of the round logo emblazoned on the building, as if to say you don't know everything. Someone poured their sweat and tears into this company and built it up from the ground. Hadn't the Society done the same? *Well, except for Finn.*

Grace Edison wasn't hard on the eyes and she might make his stay interesting. Her blonde hair barely touched her shoulders and Chase pictured running his hand through the soft tresses. When they locked eyes, he took notice of the chestnut brown color yet there was more to them. Grace had a haunted look about her or a hidden secret. "What could it be?" Chase said under his breath and placed the key in the ignition, almost forgetting how to start a car.

When the Honda had first arrived, he had searched for the remote start, then the startup button like on his Aston Martin. "Piece of junk! Shit, why did I agree to this?" He pounded the steering wheel. "Get a grip, man." Chase looked in the rearview mirror and scratched his jaw. "Come on, man. Let's find out where this adventure takes you."

After finding a spot in his apartment's parking garage, Chase took the elevator to the fifth floor.

Busy with his phone, he hadn't noticed a young woman wearing a black tank top and faded, tight jeans when he had stepped into the elevator. Swearing under his breath at the burner phone, he stuck it in his pocket.

"They can be a bitch."

Chase looked up with questioning eyes.

"Phones." The dark-haired woman rolled hers. "Sometimes I think we're better without them. Hi, I'm Darcy, by the way." She extended her hand and her dark hair slipped forward over her shoulders. "You just move in?"

"Uh, yeah. Chase. Chase Garrett." He took her hand. "Nice to meet you."

"Oh, and you're polite too."

The elevator stopped at the fourth floor. "If you're ever bored and want to hang out, I'm in four-o-eight." She winked. "You're cute."

The doors slid together, and Chase smacked his forehead. "Focus, man, focus. No Darcys allowed." He walked to his apartment. "Or Graces, either."

Chase hit the speed dial for Mr. Smith and waited while unlocking the door.

"Hello, Mr. Young."

"Mr. Smith."

"What can I do for you this evening?"

Mr. Smith must be in the area if he knew it was evening. Chase had driven around the city for most of the afternoon, treating himself to lunch and a stroll in the park to think.

"I need some of my money for an investment."

"I see."

"Not, 'I see'. You ask where you should invest it." Chase's foot began to repeatedly tap the floor. "Falcon appears to have a cash flow problem. I invest. They get back on their feet. Mission accomplished." *And not so mission impossible.*

"Not so fast, Mr. Young. I thought we agreed not to use money for a quick fix. And…you are missing the point of the assignment."

"There's a point?"

"Oh, yes. Dig deeper."

"What? Did I hear you say dig deeper?" Chase scratched his head. "Mr. Smith? Mr. Smith! Hey, are you still there?" He stared at the phone. *Call Ended.* He threw it across the room and the cell bounced off the living room's wall, leaving a black indented mark. "Dammit! Son of a bitch!"

Chase was tempted to run down a floor, knock on Darcy's door and ask her to dinner. Instead, he calmed himself down, grabbed a beer from the fridge and a frozen dinner from the freezer. He flipped on a sports channel and plunked down at the dining table at the edge of the living room, waiting for the microwave to tell him dinner was served. "At least I don't have to walk far. Five steps to the kitchen and five back. Maybe I could get used to this." He chuckled.

* * * *

"This isn't like dad to hire a new pilot and not tell us," Tim said to his sister.

"I know, right?" Grace sipped her beer as they waited for her other brother to show. "Why is Mark always late? I specifically said to meet us here at six."

"My little brother follows his own schedule, except when it comes to flying." Tim winked at her. "And, he doesn't have a wife and three kids at home. He's free as a bird or should I say falcon." He laughed at his own joke.

"He's only two years younger than you, Tim. Mark's had plenty of time to do whatever he pleases. At thirty-two it's time to settle down."

"Listen to you." Tim nudged her. "How about you go on one of those dating sites instead of always telling Mark to make a profile. Mr. Wonderful could be waiting for you, and you don't even know it."

"I already had Mr. Wonderful, Tim." Grace looked over her shoulder as if she was watching for Mark, swiping her eyes at the same time. "Besides, I'm twenty-eight. I've got plenty of time." She poured another glass of beer from the pitcher. "Let's change the subject."

"All right." Tim nodded. "I need to talk to someone who's not my wife."

Grace sucked in a deep breath and made a noise in her throat.

"What?" Tim waved his hand. "No! Do you really think so little of me?"

Grace placed her hand on his shoulder. "Sorry, of course not."

"If I told Jen what I'm about to tell you, she'd want me to go for it."

"Go for what?" Grace fidgeted in her seat. "Just spill already."

"I got an offer from a major airline for fifty grand more than what Falcon pays me."

"Oh."

"I wouldn't leave, Grace, despite what you think, but I'd like to make more money."

"And since I'm Chief Officer of Finance, besides VP of Operations, you're asking me for a raise."

Tim ran his finger along his collar, looking uncomfortable. "Yeah."

"I'll look at our numbers and get back to you."

"How are my sibs doing?" Mark's arm slipped around Grace and the other over Tim's shoulders. "Family meeting?" He scanned the table. "Where's Dad?" he asked as he slid in next to Grace.

"This one is without Dad," Grace answered, noticing how much Mark looked like their mom, lighter brown hair instead of blonde like she and Tim. He didn't get their chestnut brown eyes either, his had a golden tone to them. His smile and bone structure made her think of their mom, giving Grace a twinge of sadness.

Mark helped himself to the pitcher and Grace noticed an Omega Seamaster on his wrist.

"You got the watch you've been showing us for the past few months." Grace raised her eyebrows. *Wasn't it four thousand dollars?*

"I'd been watching for it to go on sale." Mark shrugged.

"At least it's not a Rolex," Tim said with a chuckle.

"I'm not telling you what to do with your money, but I hope you're saving some of it," Grace said.

"You're not telling me what to do?" Mark pointed at her. "Baby sister is giving Marky advice? Financial background or not, I don't need your help, Gracie."

"Hey, Mark." Tim glared at him. "She's concerned about you and wants what's best." He looked at Grace. "Time to change the subject … again."

It had been a favorite line of theirs since their teen years. When they had held secret meetings and saw their mom or dad coming, one would say, "Time to change the subject…again."

"Go ahead, big bro. Change it." Mark swallowed down half his beer and held the glass in the air.

"Jen's pregnant."

Grace thought Tim forced his smile. "I'm so happy for you, Tim," she said, patting his arm. "Tell Jen I will call her soon."

"You might finally get the boy you want," Mark said.

"Mark!" Grace elbowed him in the side.

"Don't start, sis. I always win." Mark winked.

"Not always." Grace stuck out her lower lip and gave him her puppy dog eyes.

"No cheating either." Mark laughed. "Making me feel sorry for you doesn't work anymore."

"Okay, let's get back to why I called you here," Grace said. "Dad hired a new pilot, Chase Garrett. He starts tomorrow. I have him coming in at eight-thirty to meet you. Dad wants him to fly the new Miami route."

"What?" Mark slammed his glass on the table. "I told him I wanted it!"

"Then talk to Dad. For now, I am going to let you two take the lead with this guy. He's nice, polite, and says the right things, but there's something about him. He took the job too easily and didn't flinch at the salary."

"What'd you tell him?" Tim asked, leaning forward.

"90K."

"Whoa, you low-balled him."

"See what I mean? From his credentials, he could get a job anywhere and for more money. Why Falcon?"

"He's planning a takeover? Work from the inside?" Mark teased.

"Ugh, Mark, stop it. Tell me you two will be in my office at eight o'clock tomorrow morning."

"I will," Tim replied as he slid from the stool and held up his phone. "I've got to get going. Jen says dinner is ready and, where am I?"

"You're not staying?" Grace had hoped to have dinner with both her brothers.

"You're stuck with me, sis," Mark said, and gave her a pout.

CHAPTER TWO

"It's not a job interview, you've already got it," Chase mumbled, looking through his closet for a suitable outfit. He chose a yellow polo without any logo and beige khakis. "The every man look." Every man he was not, but he needed to blend.

Chase had started coffee in his small kitchen and had bought muffins and yogurt for breakfast. After finishing, he headed for the bathroom. Staring in the mirror, putting final touches to his beard with an electric razor, Chase realized it'd been many years since he had to do things for himself. Someone took and picked up his dry cleaning, food was set on the table as soon as he arrived in the dining area and when he did have to do something on his own, he called a service or ordered on-line to be delivered.

"Chase, buddy, get your shit together. Think how it used to be when you were a struggling college kid. You're on your own again like the good old days." He threw a dirty towel on the bathroom floor. "No one's going to pick it up." He walked through the apartment, grimacing. "I'm a pig." He hadn't lived there more than a week and the place looked as if a bomb exploded. "Tonight, I'll clean."

The Honda sat waiting in the spot where he'd parked it the night before. "Sorry." He patted the trunk hood. "I'd hoped you had miraculously turned into an Aston Martin overnight."

"Ooh, you have good taste." A female voice stopped him from getting in the car.

"Yeah, I wish." Chase pointed at her. "Darcy, right?"

"You remembered. Ten points."

Chase had time to study her better, noticing the extra piercings in her ears, one at her eyebrow. Her dark hair, pulled back in a high ponytail, gave off a reddish cast, like she'd put a rinse on it. He spotted a small tattoo on her right arm, partially exposed. Today she wore a black t-shirt with tight fitting black jeans and black running shoes. Not an ounce of fat on her, and she curved in all the right places. "Could I give you a ride?"

"Well, Chase, if I'm in the parking garage, I've got my own wheels." Darcy smiled.

"Of course."

"I have breakfast shift, so I need to get going."

"You work at one of the restaurants in town?"

"Yep and bartend at the Golden Swan at night. Stop by sometime."

"I will. Have a good day." Chase tipped his head. *Darcy. A needed distraction.*

The ride to Falcon took less time than he thought. Chase glanced at the car clock. Twenty minutes early. *Should I show up ahead of time?* He made a quick decision to check out the place before heading inside to waste some minutes. Chase rounded the corner of the building when he heard voices.

"Did you fix the problem?" Chase recognized Paul's voice.

"I can only do so much, boss," an unfamiliar voice answered. "Have to take things slow so as not to raise suspicion."

"Fine, but I can't wait much longer."

Chase waited a few minutes and turned the corner. *No one's here.* He went back to the front of the building to go in the main door. His burner phone said eight-twenty-three, an appropriate time.

He heard her laugh before he saw her which made his heart skipped a beat. Chase was eager to see Grace Edison again. She sat perched on her desk, surrounded by two men, one blonder than her and the other with light brown hair. The blonde had her chestnut eyes, easy to notice from a distance. Grace wore a white silk blouse and gray pencil skirt and had her legs crossed casually at the knee. It appeared something hung around her neck on a long gold chain, hidden by the shirt.

They stopped talking when Chase stepped in the room.

"Chase!" Grace slipped from the desk and smoothed her skirt. "I'd like you to meet my brothers, Tim." She gestured to the taller of the two, the one with blonde hair. "And Mark." He was shorter than Chase or Tim and appeared to work out to the point he could be a bodybuilder.

"A pleasure," Chase said and stuck out his hand, getting a powerful grip from both. He refrained from playing the game of who had the stronger handshake. Chase had seen it done before and had been guilty of doing it.

"Excuse me?" A male voice interrupted.

Chase looked over his shoulder at a young man in dark gray coveralls with a falcon patch on the pocket standing in the threshold. Dark brown hair, average height and built, he didn't seem familiar, but Chase felt like he knew him.

"Grace, you told me to let you know as soon as I did the work on the 737. The back row of seats was replaced and securely tightened. Now people won't ask what the rattling is. No more in-flight scares." He chuckled.

"Thanks, Ray."

"Anything else you need, let me know." Ray only had eyes for Grace.

Unexpected jealousy crept through Chase. Ray and Grace had a work relationship, nothing else he was sure. Yet it bothered him. After listening to Ray speak, he recognized him. Not by his face, but voice. *He was the man talking to Paul earlier.*

Chase mulled over the conversation in his mind again. It had seemed strange, but he knew now Paul spoke with his mechanic. Did he dare think the man wanted to sabotage his airline for the insurance money?

"Chase?" Grace's voice broke into his thoughts. "Do you want to copilot today?"

"What? Yeah, sure."

"Are you okay? You appear lost in thought. If you need to attend to something, you can start tomorrow," she said as she glared at her brothers. "Like we planned."

"I'm good."

"Guys, will you take him to the uniform room? Find something suitable? We'll have a tailor work on whatever is needed, Chase. Come to my office when you get back." Grace gave him a smile he hoped meant she was looking forward to seeing him again.

"Follow me," Tim said.

"Don't forget to pick up his badge and credentials from personnel," Grace called after them.

Mark fell back to join Chase. "He literally means follow him," he said with a smirk. "You and I will drive to the airport in the company car, but Tim has to take his own in case he has to leave at a moment's notice."

Chase tried to hide his surprise. "Hard to leave quickly if you're in the air," he joked.

"I know!" Mark nudged him on the arm. "We'll get along fine. But, seriously, Tim has three kids and one on the way. Can't blame him."

"No, you can't." Chase made a mental note, wondering if Tim needed money and had something to do with the financial position Falcon was in. Smith's words came to him, "Dig deeper." *Is that what he meant? Falcon isn't floundering due to sales or marketing, perhaps someone is skimming money or tampering with the books?*

Mark and Tim were quite helpful, suiting him up with Falcon attire, briefcase and carry on. The ride to the airport was short and Mark showed his and Chase's credentials at the gate. He drove to the Falcon hangar and parked next to Tim's SUV.

"He'll need a bigger car soon." Mark chuckled. "Tim's fought buying a van, but it's a reality now."

"Does his wife work?" *Stupid question.*

"Not anymore and I don't have to tell you why. The girls are six, five and three."

"All girls." Chase nodded. He could picture himself as a dad to girls, except for dressing up as a princess.

"Estrogen city at the Timothy Edison house." Mark walked into the hangar and around the corner.

Chase hurried after him, not wanting to miss a detail. Ray sat at a table with five others who appeared to be in a meeting. "Ray's in charge here, our top mechanical tech," Mark told him. "He answers to me or Tim."

"Wasn't he just at headquarters?"

"Any chance to be in the same room with my sister, he takes it. Ray could have easily sent a text. He's like a puppy looking for a 'good dog' reaction from her."

Might as well ask. "Are they dating?"

"Ray and Grace?" Mark made a face. "No. He asked her out once and she went. Pity date."

Chase couldn't believe Grace would call it a pity date. Mark was full of himself, maybe he thought it was pity, but not her. He pictured her gently letting him down during the evening, maybe over dessert. Grace would tell Ray he was a wonderful man and hoped they'd continue to be friends.

"You must go through airport security, too, Chase," Tim said as he joined them. "Ray said Gate E34 is open and ready. He'll have the plane there in a few."

"First flight of the day for you?" Chase asked, walking alongside Tim toward the airport.

"Yeah, we take off at ten-o-five for Atlanta. It's about a forty-five-minute flight. From there we pick up passengers who've flown there and continue to Orlando. There's always someone who wants to meet Mickey Mouse."

"About an hour flight from Atlanta," Chase stated.

"Right!" Tim laughed. "I forgot I was dealing with an experienced commercial airline pilot."

Chase detected a slightly sarcastic tome and tried a quick fix. "Not too experienced. I'll need your help."

"Who did you fly with before? American?"

He's setting me up. "Continental. They're no longer flying, having merged with United. I always wanted to live in North Carolina, so I applied to Falcon."

"Where'd you live before? Continental had hubs in Houston, Denver…"

"Cleveland. I lived in Cleveland. Great place, but I was ready for a new start."

"Ever been to the Rock and Roll Hall of Fame?"

What is this? Twenty questions? "Yeah, several times. If you haven't been, you need to go." Chase decided it was time he got answers. "I thought Falcon flew direct to Orlando."

"Oh, we do." Tim nodded. "I like this route. It's an all-day there and back. I'm home by six."

"In time for supper."

Tim raised his brows. "I guess my little brother told you I'm a married man with three daughters."

"Yeah."

"What happened to your copilot? I hope I didn't bump him or her."

Tim crossed his brows. "We told you in Grace's office, my copilot had a sudden emergency. We asked if you didn't mind filling in last minute."

"Right." Chase shrugged liked he forgot. *Need to pay better attention.*

They arrived at the security checkpoint none too soon. Chase followed Tim to the TSA Precheck, whipping through the area in record time. Walking to the gate, Chase felt many pairs of eyes on them. In the past, his inner radar would zone in on any women sending a signal and find an excuse to stroll over. "Did you drop this?" he'd ask, even though he had nothing to show. A favorite line and always worked. Two good-looking guys in uniform. It made heads turn, but he kept looking straight ahead.

* * * *

"I hope my brothers treated you well." Grace lifted the corners of her mouth as she looked up from her paperwork.

"They were very helpful." Chase pointed to the seat in front of her desk. "May I?"

"Sure." Grace glanced down, frowned and looked back up at him. "I don't really know you, but can I ask you a question?"

"Of course."

"Are you good with numbers?"

Hell, yeah. I'm a numbers guy. Chase internally chuckled. "Like math, accounting?"

"Yes." Grace blew a puff of air, her lower lip jutting out. "I can't seem to find the problem."

"Since I still have to gain your trust, tell me the general problem."

Grace's eyes widened, she cocked her head and smiled. "Thanks."

Chase settled back in the chair and folded his hands over his chest. "Let's hear it."

Her smile had disappeared, and she gave him a questioning look. "First, I have to ask you something. What's up with you? Mr. Nice Guy. Always agreeable."

Chase felt like she hit him with a brick. "I'm … sorry?"

"There's something I'm missing." Grace pointed at him. "And I will find out." She broke into a smile again. "Don't look so serious, Chase. Unless it's something bad. Are you hiding a secret?"

"Are you?"

The playfulness between them was sucked out of the room. A serious tone followed. "If a company has been in the black for several years in a row, continues to fill their planes to almost capacity daily, negotiates for the best fuel prices and even has a separate account for maintenance costs, why are they in the red?"

Someone is playing with the numbers? Chase lifted his shoulders. "I'd have to look."

"You have an accounting background?" Grace tapped a pen against her lips.

Chase couldn't stop staring at those lips, kissable ones, not those fake pumped up ones he often came across during his dating adventures. He shook his head to clear his mind.

"So, you don't," Grace said.

"Not a degree, but I have a background," Chase clarified. *Banking is my middle name, sweetheart. Not the everyday, can I help you open a loan banker. Investment banking.*

With the help of the Society, each member had found their dream job to start their career. Someone always knew a person who knew another who could help. Hard work, twelve-hour days, persistence and reinvesting got him to where he was today. A billionaire.

Three years ago, he'd stepped away from the rat race to work from home. He had enough to start his dream company. His passion was flying, and the money helped him start his own private airline for the rich and famous with bases here, California and New York. Besides the flights, he ran a training school for commercial pilots in Charlotte and rented his jets to experienced ones. He hired trustworthy people, ones who'd do the work whether or not he was there.

"I've seemed to have lost you again, Mr. Garrett," Grace said. "Where *do* you go?"

Crap! She can tell? I've got to stop daydreaming.
"Nowhere. I'm thinking over your problem. I'll keep an eye out for anything suspicious."

"Thank you, it's all I can ask." Grace stood and put out her hand. "Thank you, Chase."

Chase rose from his seat and took her small, soft hand in his. "Do you ever leave this place, Ms. Edison?"

"I do."

"I've eaten no dinner yet, why don't you join me?"

"Another time, perhaps? I'm not quite finished here."

Chase clutched his chest, feigning hurt and surprise.

"I hope I didn't mortally wound you." Grace lifted one side of her mouth.

"You didn't." Chase turned to leave then pivoted in place. "How about tomorrow?" He wasn't used to being shot down by women. *Or they knew I had money? I hung out at expensive restaurants and exclusive clubs. Were they saying yes to me ... or my money?*

"I'll see you tomorrow, Chase," Grace said with a laugh and returned to her paperwork.

When Chase reached the Honda, he pounded the roof before getting in. "Damn!" He sat behind the wheel and laughed. "I take out my frustrations on you, don't I?"

As he drove home, he detoured at the light and headed for the downtown area. It was almost eight and he hadn't eaten. "I hope the Golden Swan serves food."

The bar was part of one of the quaint strip malls lining the main street. The dark brown brick building was old but well cared for. Hanging baskets hung from the lampposts and huge cement pots of flowers had been placed at street corners. The road changed to red brick right through the center of town and its side streets. Chase wondered if Grace had ever been to this part of the city.

Chase opened the door to the Golden Swan which was longer than it was wide. A few round tables were in the front window and some ran opposite of the extensive bar. Farther back were more tables and chairs and a door to the outside. A sign on the wall said "Patio - Open" with an arrow. He slid onto a barstool close to the door, spotting Darcy talking to a customer. When she looked over, he raised his hand in greeting.

Darcy took her time making her way down the bar, chatting and refilling people's beers as she walked toward Chase. "Isn't it past your bedtime, Tiger?" she asked when she finally approached. She lifted the eyebrow with the piercing.

"Not yet. Beer, please."

"Anything in particular. We've got plenty on tap."

"You choose."

Chase wondered why he'd come. In the past, Darcy would have already been in his bed and he would meet up with her on a casual basis. As she strolled toward him, he realized he needed a friend. Chase swallowed hard.

"You okay, Tiger?" Darcy placed a hand on her hip, beer in the other.

Can everyone read my mind in this damn town? "Yeah, fine. You got time to talk?"

Darcy looked over her shoulder. "It's Tuesday. A slow day. How about if I put in an order for you? Burger?"

"Sounds great." Chase sipped his beer, a good craft one, while he waited for her to come back.

"How old are you?" he asked when she returned.

"Whoa, there." She held up her hands. "Are you an undercover cop or something?"

"No." He chuckled.

"If I'm bartending, I'm legal." Darcy stared at him. "Guess."

"Twenty-two."

"Add a year." She wiped the bar with a towel.

Right up his alley. Young enough to not want marriage and just have a good time. He should be jumping all over this. "Want to be friends?"

Darcy smacked the bar with the towel and let out a whoop. "What are you? Five?"

Chase leaned toward her. "I kind of feel that way. I'm new in town."

Darcy's face changed to a serious look. "I find it hard to believe you don't have any friends."

"Not here."

"So, call them."

"I can't. I'm not allowed."

"Wow, you really are five."

"Well?"

"Well, what?"

"Friends?" Chase gave her his best smile.

"You don't want to date or get me in bed?"

"No … well yes, of course, you are hot and sexy…"

"I'm teasing. Friends is nice. I never had a guy ask me to be a friend. Besides, I was going to tell you, you're too old for me. What are you, like thirty-five?" She teased.

"What?" Chase ran his hand through his hair.

"Watch it, Perfect. You'll mess the do."

"What happened to Tiger?"

"That was before you wanted to be friends. Now, you get a new name."

"You think I'm perfect?" Chase didn't know if he should take it as a compliment or not.

"Look at you." Darcy waved her hand. "Not a hair out of place, you trim your beard probably twice a day and I'm sure you work out daily. If you've been on the job all day, your clothes look freshly pressed."

Chase winced at how spot-on she was. "I'm a pilot. I wear a uniform."

"And the girls go crazy," Darcy jiggled her hands in the air. "Am I right?" She lifted the pierced brow again.

"I just started. I'll tell you tomorrow when I stop for dinner."

"How do you know I'll be working?"

"If not, I'm come to your apartment. Four-o-eight, right?"

"I'll be here, so don't go knocking on my door."

"Good to know." Chase winked as a burger was slid in front of him.

CHAPTER THREE

Grace walked to her window and stared out at the parking lot. She'd been in the office since seven a.m. trying to work. Instead of getting anything done, she'd been glancing at the window every five minutes, watching for him so she finally gave up and stood by it. When she saw Chase hop from his car, she made a beeline back to her desk, pretending to be busy. *What am I doing?* She scolded herself. He'd awoken something inside her, a buried feeling she never thought she'd experience again.

"Good morning, Grace."

She took her time pulling her eyes away from the computer screen and asked, "Ever been to Miami?"

Grace sat waiting, thinking the time he took too long to speak. *What's with this guy? Is he rehearsing his answer?*

"Sure. Hasn't everyone?" Chase broke into one of his killer smiles, making her forget her suspicions.

"Spring break, right?"

"Did you ever go?"

"Once." Grace lifted her shoulder. She wouldn't give away too many personal details to this mysterious man. Not until she knew more about him. *What am I thinking?* She bit into her bottom lip. *He did ask me out.* "The Miami run debuts tomorrow. First flight leaves at eight a.m. Paul wants you to pilot and Tim will pick your copilot." At work, she always called her dad, Paul, still foreign sounding after seven years, as if he was some co-worker instead of her father. "There will be a bit of fanfare. The press will be there, and Paul will cut the ribbon." *Did he fidget in his seat?*

"Sounds great."

"Paul usually goes on the first trip, but he has a meeting with an investor. I volunteered to take his place. You'll make two runs, morning and one in the afternoon. Paul will go over the details with you. Do you know where his office is?"

"I think I can find it."

"Where did you go for dinner last night? Anywhere good?" Grace asked, getting a slight reaction from Chase.

"The Golden Swan, a bar with food. Ever heard of it?"

"I can't say I have."

"A friend of mine works there. She told me to stop by anytime."

"Oh." Grace spun in her chair to face her computer screen. Why were her hands trembling? She had no right to be jealous.

"She's a friend," Chase said as if reading her mind and stood. "I'll be on my way if it's okay with you. See you tomorrow?"

Grace looked up into his chocolate eyes, lost for a moment in the deliciousness. "Yes, come here to my office first thing. I'll go with you to the airport."

"May I ask the gate number…in case I'm late or caught in traffic?"

"The E concourse for sure, all the way to the end. I have yet to get the number."

"On second thought," Chase said from the doorway. "I'll head straight there. Don't wait for me."

"Sounds like a plan," Grace said with too big of a smile. *He's blowing me off. The friend must have become more than someone to meet at a bar and have drinks.* "Damn! I should have gone to dinner." She slapped the desk, took a breath and gave her attention to the computer screen.

* * * *

Chase cringed after he ran his hand through his hair and reviewed his list once more. *Mess hair. Check. Coffee with lid. Check. Loosen lid later. Start to jog when I reach E concourse. Check.* His picture in a local newspaper might blow his cover. Chase wondered how Paul hadn't recognized him, both being part of the local airline scene. *Paul might know the name, not the face. You're not going by Chase Young.* He smirked. *I never heard of Paul either.*

It was hard to get Grace out of his mind since they'd talked yesterday. She flirted yet held back. He'd watched her finger the silver chain around her slender neck during their conversation. Whatever she hid, the answer was at the end of the necklace. When she mentioned Miami would be his route, he almost did a dance. Nash, a Society member, lived there, and maybe he'd sneak a message to meet up at the airport. He'd have about an hour before heading back to Charlotte. It would be great to see a friendly face, if only for a short time. Mr. Smith would never know unless Chase was under surveillance twenty-four seven.

However, a visit with Nash would have to take place another day. Grace would fly on the inaugural trip and he planned to make the most of it. When back in Charlotte, after the first flight, he'd suggest lunch. He wished they could stay in Miami and go to Miami Beach since he knew the place so well.

The E concourse loomed ahead. Chase took a breath, ready for his big scene. *Showtime.* He picked up speed, dodging rolling luggage and passengers. He glanced at a large clock on the wall, wanting to time his entrance perfectly. A small crowd had gathered around

Gate 33. *It has to be the one. Paul said he got passes for reporters.*

"Chase! Where have you been?" Grace sounded out of breath. Her cheeks flushed pink as she rushed toward him.

"Sorry, I got stuck in the Starbucks line. Didn't realize the time." He held up his java and when he brought it down, popped the lid.

"I want you to meet your copilot then pose for pictures with Paul, you and Halle on either side of him." Grace waved to a petite African American woman, looking fit and trim, wearing the same uniform. He'd guess she was early thirties and noticed she wore a wedding ring.

"Halle will be your second-in-command, Chase. She's reliable, been flying with us for five years and is one damn good tennis player."

Chase shook hands. "You play with Grace?"

"Yes, but don't let her fool you. She's a great player." Halle appeared to be sizing him up. "What about you? You look as if you'd play."

"Sometimes." Chase shrugged, picturing his court in the backyard of his compound, wanting to offer the women free reign any time they wished to play.

Grace stood close by him, making the setting for his plan workable. After dropping Halle's hand, he stepped back into Grace. The coffee lid flew from the cup and he helped matters by tipping it toward him.

"Oh, Chase! I am so sorry." Grace covered her mouth.

Halle dashed into the closest women's restroom and returned before he blinked. "Here." She pushed the towels against his chest.

"Thanks." Chase looked over his shoulder. "I better clean up in the men's room."

"You'll miss the ceremony and pictures," Grace moaned.

"I'm sure Halle will do a fine job. She can represent both of us." Chase nodded at her and rushed for the safety of the men's bathroom.

Once he was sure the photographers and reporters had retreated down the concourse, Chase made his appearance.

"I hope this isn't a sign of bad luck," Paul said with a laugh and patted Chase on the back.

"No, it's me being clumsy. I should have waited on the coffee."

"No, you shouldn't have," Halle answered. "Airline coffee?" She made a face. "Sometimes you have to take what you get." She glanced at her watch. "Time to board, Captain."

As he passed by Grace, she ran her hand down his arm. "Have a safe trip."

Chase pulled his brows together. "I thought you were coming."

"I am. I always say it to the pilot if I'm at the airport."

"Then you have a safe trip, too." Chase winked. "Where will you sit?"

"First row. Now, get going. Halle's waiting."

Once on board, Halle introduced Chase to the three flight attendants. Nothing seemed amiss, the 737 had 137 seats, so according to regulations, three were needed. Sue Ann appeared to be in charge, an older woman with short gray hair and a deep tan. Peter seemed the youngest, pale with freckles, tall and red-haired. June was a fortyish black woman with perfect makeup who greeted him warmly.

"I serve the pilots," June said as she shook Chase's hand. "Can I get you anything before the passengers come aboard?"

Chase thought of the coffee story. "Thank you, I'm fine. But Halle would like some." He felt a nudge in his back and chuckled.

"Come on, big guy." Halle tugged the back of his jacket. "Places, everyone, they're letting the dogs out."

The crew was personable and humorous, but once the passengers arrived, professionalism kicked into high gear, except when Peter sang a rousing rendition of Frank Sinatra's "Come Fly with Me" to get their attention before instructing the people on safety regulations.

The time in the air had been smooth, and the touchdown was one of Chase's best. No air pockets, not one jostle of the plane. He shook hands with Halle after the landing. "Great job." He thanked the people for flying with Falcon Airlines and stood in the doorway with Halle, nodding at passengers as they filed by to disembark. Chase pinned wings on a few children who asked, answered questions from budding weather people and aviation students, and finally retreated to the cockpit.

"We couldn't have asked for better weather," Grace said over his shoulder. She was close enough for him to catch a scent of her perfume.

Chase stood, almost bumping into her and sniffed the air. "Magnolias?"

Grace smelled his jacket. "Coffee?"

"Very funny. I need to stretch my legs. How about if we walk the concourse, find a café?"

"We're in Terminal F. I know a place."

They walked almost to the entrance of the concourse to Café Versailles and Grace ordered two Cuban coffees and two breakfast empanadas. "This should hold us until the flight back."

Chase glanced around for a place to sit. They strolled to the closest gate and found two seats away from the crowd. "Thanks for breakfast. Lunch is on me."

Grace turned away from her food and lifted her brows. "Oh, really?"

"Yes, I would like to take you out to lunch."

"I would love it."

* * * *

Chase hoped the service had delivered the picnic basket and quilt to Falcon Headquarters. He told Grace he needed to swing by the building before lunch. Although his money was in a trust, he got an allowance and would keep any money made from his job. They had a two-hour window of time and he planned to make the most of it.

"Freedom Park, here we come!" he called when he returned to the car from picking up lunch.

When Grace saw the picnic basket her eyes lit with pleasure. "I haven't been to Freedom Park in so long and it's right in the city. What a wonderful idea!"

Chase loaded the basket in the trunk and headed toward the park. It thrilled him Grace thought lunch there was better than an upscale restaurant in the city. Besides, if he showed his face in one, they'd call him Mr. Young. *Not good.* "We'll sit anywhere you want," he said as they walked on the paved walkway.

"By the lake," Grace answered.

Chase spread the quilt on the grass and Grace helped by pulling at the corners until it lay flat.

"This is more than just lunch," Grace said, kneeling in front of the basket and peeking inside. She looked young and happy in a yellow cotton dress, sprinkled with flowers around the edge of the skirt. He was glad she hadn't chosen a pencil skirt today. The dress she wore flowed around her legs as she knelt over the basket. "Tiny sandwiches with no crusts!" she squealed in delight. "I haven't had those in ages."

Chase joined her on the blanket and pulled a bottled of fresh sweetened tea from the cooler side of the basket. "Hope you like tea. It's my favorite." He poured some into the pale green heavy-duty plastic cups embossed with suns around the middle of the glass.

"You've used this service before, I can tell," Grace said, lifting the cup to her lips. "We will not throw these out. They're nicer than some I've seen in stores."

"And matching plates." Chase nodded toward the inside of the basket.

"I feel completely spoiled." Grace sat, leaned back on one hand and looked up at the sky.

"I have a feeling you don't pamper yourself often," Chase said.

Grace lifted her sunglasses, giving him a quizzical stare. "What do you mean?"

"You seem to put your brothers' and father's needs before yours. What have they done for you lately?"

"My brothers go out to dinner with me when I ask…well, Mark does. Tim stays for drinks and appetizers, then goes home."

"And your dad?"

"He's overwhelmed lately." Grace pursed her lips.

"You look like you have something more to say," Chase prodded.

"He's concerned about me, like any good father. When you came to Falcon, he told me to be open to new possibilities."

"Are you?"

"Yes," she whispered.

Chase' heart skipped a beat. He took her tea, set it on the basket lid which served as a tray, and brushed her lips with his. "Like this?"

"Um." Grace bit into her bottom lip. "I think that is what he meant."

"I am open to new possibilities, too." Chase kissed her once more, a chaste yet satisfying one.

Grace pulled back and gazed into his eyes. "To be continued? We need to eat and get to the airport."

* * * *

Her heart beat fast in her chest, making it almost impossible to think. Awkward silences filled part of the ride back to the airport then at other times easy conversation. Grace couldn't stop thinking about the kiss. She didn't want to be naïve yet had to find the courage to ask if he was single. Chase might have a family stashed away in Cleveland for all she knew. People lied on applications all the time.

"Is something wrong?" Chase asked on their walk down the concourse. "You seem fine one minute and the next…"

"Do you have a girlfriend?" Grace blurted out. "Or a wife?"

Chase chuckled. "No."

"You said you had a friend who worked at a bar," Grace answered, making quotation marks with her fingers when she said the word friend.

"Darcy? Nah., she lives in my building. I meet her in the elevator and since I was new here, we clicked as friends."

"Oh."

"Not, oh." Chase stopped in the middle of the concourse, placed a finger under her chin and tipped her head toward him. "I'm having feelings for a woman I recently met, and she's standing in front of me."

Grace held back a gasp and told her heart to stop jumping into her stomach and back again. "I may share those same feelings," she whispered.

"Let's see where this goes," Chase said. "We'll go fast, slow, whatever speed you want."

"I'd like that." Grace followed him into the skybridge and onto the plane. "I'll be right here." She pointed to the first row, first seat by the aisle.

Halle came aboard, and they chatted while the flight attendants made last-minute preparations.

"Do you like him?" Grace whispered to Halle.

"As a person or a pilot, Grace?" Halle's smirk turned into a smile. "Oh, wait a minute! You like him. Good for you! It's about time."

"You didn't answer the question, Halle."

"I hardly know the man. I can tell you he is an excellent pilot. Your dad made the right decision hiring him."

"You were locked in there for three hours, Hal. Come on, you have an opinion."

"On the flight down, we asked the usual questions. You know, how many women, or men, have you slept with, did you ever flunk a class or cheat on a test."

"Halle!" Grace giggled. "Did you find out?"

Halle gave her a quick hug. "Not yet, maybe on this flight. Get in your seat now and use the seatbelt."

The first passengers boarding the aircraft ended their conversation. Grace sat down, trying to stay out of the way. Gazing out the window, she thought the day seemed brighter and she felt happier than in a long time. *Don't get carried away! It was just a kiss. No, it was a wonderful kiss.* Nothing would ruin her almost perfect day.

Halfway through the smooth flight, Grace noticed June knocking on the cabin door then let herself in. Ten minutes later, she slipped out again. The suspense was killing her. She unbuckled her seatbelt and walked to the attendant station. "Is everything all right, June?"

"A few passengers were complaining to Peter. I relayed his message to the pilots."

Peter sat in the back of the plane and worked from the station set up there. Grace glanced down the aisle and he wiggled his fingers in a wave as if to say he was fine. "Please, keep me in the loop."

"I will." June nodded.

"We will begin the descent in a few minutes, folks," a male voice came over the speakers. "Another twenty minutes, we'll be in Miami. A cool eighty-nine degrees. Please, return to your seats, fasten your seatbelts and prepare for landing."

A tingle traveled down Grace's spine when she heard Chase's voice. But other voices made her turn her head. Far in the back of the plane, people were shouting. Sue Ann and Peter were doing their best to calm the situation. June left her station and headed down the aisle to assist her colleagues.

No! This can't be happening. We don't want trouble on our first day. Grace clutched her hands together and stayed turned, watching from her seat. She tried to gage what was happening. *A drunken passenger? I can't believe I'm thinking this, but please be a drunken passenger.*

"We're going down!" a voice screamed. "The tail's about to crack!"

CHAPTER FOUR

Shouts and screams came down the aisle in a ripple effect. Babies began to cry, women shrieked or moaned, and men hollered or swore, some tried to jump from their seats. June rushed down the aisle toward the front, and Grace let out the breath she held. "What?" she yelled over the shouting voices. "Tell me."

"We're fine. A nervous passenger heard a strange rattle and reported it to Peter. I let the pilots know, and we decided it was nothing. Chase said they will check it after we landed. The whole back row says their seats are shaking, rocking and rolling. They're afraid the tail is about to break off. We tried to calm their fears, but they won't stop shouting."

"Find them new seats."

"We're working on it." June widened her eyes. "Poor Paul. He didn't need this to happen on the first day."

"How much longer until we land?"

"Ten minutes?" June lifted a shoulder. "I need to talk to Chase and Halle." She patted Grace's arm. "It will be okay."

Okay? Grace looked at the frightened faces around her and the crowd standing in the back of the plane. The noise level had dropped but the voices sounded loud and angry. Peter tried to shout above them, telling them to please take their seats.

"Hello, this is your captain," A voice announced over the speakers. "I can assure you the tail will not fall off the plane and the noise you hear may have something to do with wind shifts causing something inside the plane to rattle. I checked all the engines, and they are fine. Please find your seats, we are about to land."

Shouts of joy erupted from the back of the plane. To Grace, it sounded as if this was the worst experience on an airline they'd ever had, and they were grateful to escape with their lives. Soon social media would be flooded with their stories, true or not. She had to get ahead of the rumors but had no access until they landed.

The wheels hit the tarmac and Grace instantly dialed her dad's number.

"What's going on, Gracie? I was just informed Facebook, Twitter and all those other outlets I can't keep up with are abuzz with the safe landing of our plane after a scare in the air, dammit! That's the hashtag, in case you're interested. Scare in the air."

"I don't know what happened yet, Dad. I suggest you send another plane down here for the last flight back today. I'll stay with this one and find out what happened."

"I'll put a call into my man down there and let you know our designated hangar once I talk to him. Since we're new to the scene, it may be awhile. I'll text you as soon as I find out."

"I can't believe this happened, Dad."

"Try to stay calm, Dumpling. As long as you're all right, I can handle the rest."

"I'm fine. Don't worry about me."

"As soon as you know the problem, get an explanation on our Facebook page and whatever else you kids use."

"I will…and, Dad, I am so sorry."

"It's not your fault. Love you." He ended the call.

Grace's heart broke for him. The bad press would not help Falcon's bottom line and it'd take double the good press to squash the rumors. *Hashtag, scare in the air.*

She shook her head. How quickly people can get a message started, good or bad.

Once the door opened to the skywalk, people pushed and shoved to get off the plane. Grace heard mumbles of "We'll never fly Falcon again" to "I want my money back", cringing at every negative comment. She made a mental note. *We must offer some type of voucher.*

The crew assembled in front of the cockpit after the last person deplaned.

"What the hell happened?" Chase stormed out of the small room toward the back of the plane. He sat in the last row of seats and shook the chair. Without notice, the row tipped backward, making an awful squawking noise before he caught himself. Chase hopped up and made eye contact with Grace. "Grace, find out which plane was assigned to us."

Grace knew exactly what he meant. Ray had fixed the back row of seats in a 737 and put it back in rotation. Her fingers flew across the keyboard, texting Ray and her dad to ask if Chase was assigned the repaired plane. Silence filled the cabin as they waited. A slight ding from her phone alerted her to a response.

"It's Ray." Her hand holding the phone was trembling and Chase wrapped his around her wrist for support.

"Whatever happens, it will be all right," he whispered.

How does he know? He can't predict the future. Grace read the message aloud. "Yes, it is the one."

"He did a damn good job of fixing them!" Chase jiggled the seats with his hand and bent down for a closer inspection. "Didn't Ray say he installed new seats and made sure they were bolted tight? Look at these. The material is worn if you look closely. They are definitely not new. And the bolts?" He gestured to the floor. "I'm not getting down there, but I'm sure they're loose."

"What?" Grace's heart pounded. *Why would someone try to sabotage the plane?* She looked at the flight attendants. "Thanks for all your help today. You were great. If I was in your place, I have no idea how I would've handled screaming passengers. You're the trained professionals, and I'm so glad we hired each one of you." She hugged the attendants. "You don't have to stay on board. Another plane is on its way and you can go back with it."

June squeezed her hand. "Paul will be on the flight from Charlotte."

Strange. She knows before I did. Has she been in contact with Dad? Wait… Grace's eyes welled with tears as a realization struck her. She suspected her dad had been dating someone and now she knew. She was glad it was June.

"I can stay with you, Grace."

"No, you should be there for Dad. Try to keep him calm." Grace pulled June to one side. "Why didn't you tell me you were dating him," she said under her breath.

"We thought it best to keep it quiet since I worked for the airline. Paul wanted no one to accuse me of getting special treatment. When I got the Miami assignment, we decided it was time to tell you and the boys."

"I am happy for both of you, but if it gets serious, all bets are off. I'm telling the world, Falcon be damned. Your personal lives come first." Grace smiled. "Do me a favor?"

"Anything."

"Get Peter and Sue Ann off the plane and convince my dad to go back with you tonight."

"The first is easy … but your dad?"

"Please? Tell him I've got this. I want to sort this out myself. He has enough pressure on him."

"True." June tapped her lips with a finger. "I'll try my best. You take care, Grace. I know you've got this."

Halle approached after June left the aircraft. "I got a message from Paul. Hangar's ready. Chase!" she called. "Let's get this baby to bed."

"Halle, did my dad say if he was coming?"

"Yeah, he did."

"Okay, we'll wait for him in the hangar."

＊ ＊ ＊ ＊

Chase was glad to hear Paul would arrive shortly. He had a lot of questions, the first being why did he want to sabotage his own company? The conversation he'd heard a few days ago might be the proof he needed and a place to start. Chase would confront Paul with this information. Hopefully Paul's explanation would get off his growing list of suspects. *Not in front of Grace. I must wait for the right time.*

"Dad!" Grace rushed to Paul as he entered the hangar.

"What the hell happened?" Paul asking, removing the Falcon baseball cap from his head.

Chase let Grace take the lead. She told the facts without getting dramatic. "Right, Chase?"

"I was in the cockpit during most of it, but Grace has told you how I remember it."

"I'd like to check the plane and talk to the mechanic on duty," Paul said.

Chase watched Grace walk away with her dad, deep in conversation. She left him at the mechanic's door with a hug. When she returned, Chase said, "I need to go over some things with Paul … alone. If you don't mind."

"No, go ahead, I need to get on our social media sites and put out fires. The report is good, except for a loose row of seats." Grace pulled her brows together. "Strange. Ray said he fixed them, and I trust his word."

"Then make it right." Chase wrapped his hand around her forearm. "When you're done, since we're stuck in Miami, I thought we might do something."

"It's terrible to be stuck in Miami." Grace rolled her eyes playfully. "I already booked rooms at the airport hotel for us."

Chase hesitated to tell her he'd ordered a rental car, and it was on its way to the hotel. He wanted to take her to dinner in Miami Beach. "Sounds great. I shouldn't be long." He had watched out of the corner of his eye for Paul and the mechanic to go to the plane and waited until the mechanic came down the stairs. He made his move, taking the steps two at a time. "Paul?"

"Here, Chase."

Good, he's in the back of the plane. "Checking the seats?"

"They seem fine, but we'll still have you fly it back in the morning instead of tonight. I might try to find a few passengers to fill it." Paul ran his hand through his dark blonde hair which showed signs of graying. "I grabbed Halle's husband on the way down and they're checking into the hotel. Maybe you four could have dinner?"

What is he? Match dot com? Chase shook his head. *Get back on track. Confront him.* "Paul, I was at Falcon when Ray reported he had repaired the seats. I examined them, and they aren't brand new."

"He never said they were new, did he? But, you're right. They're not new."

This is too easy. He's confessing? "You admit you deceived your daughter when Ray told her new seats were installed?"

"No, I did not deceive my daughter or anyone. These are new seats, refurbished second-hand ones. I'd told Ray to buy on the secondary market when it didn't come down to safety or maintenance of the engines."

"I heard you ask Ray if he fixed the problem."

"The seats, Chase." Paul rubbed his face. "Shit! Were you spying on us? I take it you listened to everything and jumped to your own conclusions?"

"Yeah, sorry, it happened a few days ago by accident, I swear, but I heard Ray say something like 'I can only do so much. I need to take things slow, so we don't raise suspicions'."

"God, man! Don't you know not to eavesdrop? Nothing good comes of it."

"Are you going to take me out back and shoot me?" Chase lifted a brow.

"Dammit, no! Ray and I were talking about Grace. The girl catches everything in the reports. If she saw a company's name repeatedly in one month's time Grace would want to check into it, find out what they sell. Then she'd look for a better price. I can confirm this practice. She's done it in the past. So, if she looked into this, she'd discover we were cutting corners and have a lot of questions. I thought it best if it stayed between Ray and me."

"Okay, you explained one question I had." Chase folded his arms over his chest. "But how you answered him causes some doubt."

Paul's face had turned a deep shade of red, and he shook with rage. "You're making a lot of assumptions, Chase! You think I'd sabotage my company?"

"Do you, Chase?" Grace's quivering voice came from the front of the plane.

"We're not done here," Chase said to Paul under his breath and turned to face Grace. "No, we were discussing different possibilities. I was talking hypothetical."

"Oh." She spun and headed for the exit.

"Grace! Wait!" Chase looked at Paul. "I have more questions."

"*If* you *still* have a job," Paul snarled.

You'll lose the girl and the job, asshole! "Look, Paul, can we continue this later … in a calm manner? If you're in trouble, I want to help."

"Come to my office when you get back tomorrow. We'll discuss what's happened, and I'll make my decision if you'll stay on or not."

Job be damned. Chase rushed toward the exit, skidding to a stop. *You'll lose everything.* He ran down the stairs in time to catch sight of Grace leaving the hangar. *You can make the money back. You did it once before.* "Grace!"

Chase sprinted across the hangar's concrete floor. Grace turned one more corner which would take her toward the airport. Picking up speed, he caught up, snatched her by the arm, and placed her between the hangar's outside wall and his body. "Let me explain."

* * * *

Grace gasped in surprise by the sudden jerk to her body. Caught between Chase and a wall she inhaled spices mixed with his own manly scent. Her knees weakened, and she fought to keep her weakness in check. *Who does he think he is?* She lifted her arms and pushed at his chest. He didn't move.

"If I back up, will you listen?"

Grace nodded.

"You asked me to help you out, and I did. Paul thought I accused him of sabotaging his own company and had a right to be angry. When we get back from Miami, I'll talk to him again, make it right."

"If you have a job." Grace smirked.

"And that." Chase grinned. "You sound just like him, you know? But right now, all I care about is you. Can we put this aside till we get back to Charlotte? I'd much rather take you to dinner."

His face, inches from her own, made thinking difficult. In the moment, Grace didn't care about work and lifted her chin, so their lips almost touched. He kissed her hard, making her head spin, and when he pulled away, she wanted to grab onto him and never let go. *Why does he make me feel this way?* She leaned back and shook out her hair. "One dinner."

"Paul suggested we dine with Halle and her husband, but I'm sure they'll be fine without us."

"They won't mind at all. I may need to do a little shopping first." Grace placed her palm on his chest. "Are you going to wear the uniform?"

"I always come prepared with a change of clothes."

"I bet you do."

Instead of heading to the airport, Grace walked to the edge of the parking lot. "I called a service to take me to the hotel. It should be here any minute now."

"I'm having a car delivered to the hotel," Chase said, following her into the backseat of a car which had pulled up to the curb. "We're driving to Miami Beach tonight."

"Sounds lovely."

"We'll have a quiet night, the two of us."

Grace hoped she looked calm and gave him an approving smile. Inside, her stomach tightened into a ball, her throat constricted, and it took effort to breathe normally. Her hand instinctively flew to the chain around her neck, and she took it between two fingers, gently rolling it back and forth.

"You do it a lot," Chase said.

"What?"

"Touch the chain."

"Old habit."

"I feel there's more to it, but whenever you're ready." Chase lifted his brows.

Never. "If I tell you my secrets, you'll have to tell me yours," Grace purred. *Ooh, that came out wrong. Sounded like flirting.*

The car pulled up in front of the hotel. The couple slid from the backseat, checked in and found they were on the same floor.

"What time do you want to leave?" Grace asked, checking her watch.

"Six. Reservations are at seven."

"Gives me time to shop. Come to my room when you're ready." She hurried down the hall toward her room, opened the door and flopped on the bed. "What am I doing? I'll tell you my secrets if you tell me yours?" She smirked. "Ugh. He must think I'm sixteen."

Grace sat up and dug in her handbag for her cell. She shot off a quick text to Halle, letting her know she had checked in and would go to dinner with Chase. She finished with, "Heard Kyle flew down. Have a good time." She sent it off to text heaven and waited.

The response ding came back right away and said, "You, too.", followed by five emojis of a smiling face blowing kisses.

The next message would be harder. "Dad, I don't think Chase meant to accuse you of sabotaging the company. Hear him out. Going out to dinner with him tonight." She cringed as she sent the message. "I should have said I know about June." Grace let out a breath. "I'll save it for another day."

Staying at the airport hotel had its perks. Grace looked up stores in the concourses, searching for a summer cocktail dress and put in a call. Soon she had a few dresses, heels, and lingerie delivered to her door. She picked the one marked 'illusion sheath dress' on its tag and threw it over her head. A short black silky sheath clung to her body with a scooped neckline rounded enough to show cleavage. It hung barely to mid-thigh. The reason they called it an illusion dress was the see-through swirling pattern of black and white lace, the top layer over the black tight-fitting slip. Sleeveless, it hugged her body to the waistline and flowed out from there, touching her knees. Strappy black heel completed the look.

"Not bad," Grace backed up almost to the wall to view herself in the full-length closet mirror. "Now take it all off, shower and put it back on."

Six o'clock sharp, a knock came at the door. "Grace?"

Grace looked through the peephole to double-check. Chase stood in the hallway in a pale blue polo, cream-color khakis and boat shoes. She wondered what he smelled like, knowing he'd just stepped out of the shower.

"Grace, are you all right?" Chase looked concerned, making her heart flip.

"Yes," she said and pulled back the door.

"You look amazing." His gaze started at her feet and ended with a meeting of their eyes. "Everyone will be jealous of my date." He offered his arm to escort her to the car.

The half hour drive ended too quickly. Grace let go of work-related issues and focused on her date with a handsome man. They laughed and talked about trivial things, a wonderful departure from her everyday existence.

"Have you been here before?" Chase asked as they pulled into the parking lot of an oceanfront restaurant.

"I can't say I have." Grace shook her head. *Chase seems at home. Like he's been here more than once.* "I've been here mostly on business."

"Let's change it." Chase hopped from the driver's seat and strode around the front of the car to help her out, giving the valet his keys and twenty dollars.

The hostess guided them to a table on the patio. "I hope this fits your request, Mr. *Garrett.*"

"Absolutely," Chase answered, slipping a bill into her hand.

Isolated, yet part of the diners, Grace felt as if they had the deck to themselves. "You're very comfortable here, Chase."

"Yes, I confess, I come here every time I visit."

"So, you've been here more than a few crazy spring breaks."

"Guilty as charged."

Jamaican music played in the background, and the outdoor bar was crowded with patrons. Grace enjoyed people watching. One group of men caught her attention, young, handsome, and out for an enjoyable evening. She'd stop noticing men years ago, but since Chase Garrett had come into her life, she felt alive again.

"Enjoying the scenery?" Chase asked.

"What? Oh … yes, the ocean is beautiful. I hope we stay until sunset." They were on the east coast and there wouldn't be a sunset show over the water. Yet, watching it grow darker, staring at the ocean with Chase appealed to her.

"Chase? Hey, buddy, is that you?"

Grace watched his face harden, jaw clench and his eyes turn cold as he looked up at the visitor to their table.

"Aren't you supposed to be on assignment? Not wining and dining beautiful women."

"Hello, Nash." Chase stood. "May I introduce you to Grace Edison."

Although not her type, Grace flushed with heat. Nash was easy on the eyes with dark shaggy hair, brown eyes flecked with gold and a day's worth of stubble on his chiseled face. He wore a tight, white t-shirt showing off well-toned muscles with board shorts and sandals. Two rows of Chinese characters had been tattooed down one arm. She took his warm hand in hers, feeling his strength. "Nice to meet you."

"Grace, do you mind if I talk to Nash privately?" Chase asked. "Give me a minute."

CHAPTER FIVE

"What the fuck, man! You almost blew my cover," Chase said through gritted teeth.

"Great to see you, too, S.B.," Nash said with a chuckle. "Get it? Secret Billionaire?"

"Not funny."

Nash stared over at the table. "I thought we said no women."

"We did. She works for Falcon. What are you doing here anyway?"

"I should ask you the same question," Nash said under his breath. "This is my place."

"Not on a Thursday night."

"I brought some guys for happy hour. We worked hard at the gym today. Some of them may get franchises if I like their work ethic and don't get too drunk."

"When did not getting too drunk become a work qualification?" Chase joked.

"Hey, you better get back. Ms. Edison is giving me the eye. I think she likes me."

"She doesn't. She barely likes me."

Nash threw his head back and laughed. "When does that ever happen? You've been a chick magnet from the day I met you. If you need help smoothing things over, I'll be in the dining room." He slapped Chase on the back. "Sorry for almost blowing your cover." Nash strolled back to the bar, motioned to the guys he came with and walked inside, giving Chase a nod.

SB. Our code. Secret Billionaire. I'd love to tell Grace about it. Chase slid back into his seat, diagonal from Grace and said, "Nash and I were casual friends in college. We run into each other now and then. He owns a chain of fitness clubs, based out of Miami." He inwardly cringed at telling white lies and scratched the side of his jaw. He *had* accused Paul of sabotage, and Nash was one of his best friends, not a casual acquaintance.

"What assignment was he talking about?"

"The Miami run. I texted him when I got it. I thought we'd meet up one day. I told him it'd be short because we turn around and fly back the same day."

"Oh." Grace reached for her water glass.

"Sorry, we should order drinks. Appetizers, too?" He winked.

"Yes, I want it all." Grace's smile made him want to buy her anything in the world.

After someone took their order, Grace kept staring at him.

"What?"

"I want to know all about Chase Garrett. Don't give me the resume version, either." Grace pointed at him, glass of sangria in hand.

Okay, where do I start?" he teased. *Always tell the truth or close to it as the saying goes. It won't get you in trouble and you don't have to remember the lies.* "My parents divorced when I was five."

"I'm sorry."

"Don't be. Dad was one of those deadbeat dads. Home a few nights a week, Mom struggled to make ends meet and when there was a windfall, he gambled it away."

"Your dad was a gambler, a tough addiction. It can ruin families."

"It ruined mine." Chase wrapped his hands around his beer glass and leaned on the table edge. "Don't look so sad. There's a happy ending. Mom got a divorce, worked two jobs and met her present husband, Red, when she got a good inside sales job at a company. They married when I was seven."

"Red?" Grace touched her hair.

"Yep, don't know why people nickname someone with red hair, Red. His real name is Allan. They have a daughter, my sister Ella, who's eight years younger than me. Sweet kid. She's twenty-two, in her last year of college and ready to graduate." Chase tapped his chin. "Or she did. She didn't want to go to the ceremony, so I lost track of the exact day."

"I can't help asking. Does she have red hair?"

"Copper. She's a beauty, could be a model."

"Do you have a picture?"

Burner phone. No pics. "I got a new phone and haven't had time to transfer. When I do, I'll show you the whole family, even the gambler." Chase hadn't meant to call his dad the gambler in front of her, it popped out of his mouth before he had time to think. He'd given him the name in college. "What does your dad do?" Someone would ask him. "He gambles." Chase always answered, and everyone would laugh.

"Sorry." Grace gave him a sympathetic look.

"He tracks me down when he needs money. It's the only time I lay eyes on the man."

"Did he ever get help?"

Typical response. He'd heard it before but always forced himself to be polite. "Never." Chase pointed to himself. "I'm his ATM."

"Don't be!" Her eyes flared in anger. "He's taking advantage of you."

"Now I have a new job and moved, he's got to track me down again and it may take time." Chase smiled. It appeared Grace was on his side. She had no idea he could give his dad a thousand dollars without blinking an eye. He'd done it once too often, and she was right. Time to stop.

"Good!" Grace looked indignant for both, and Chase chuckled. "What?"

"You," he answered. "Thanks for looking out for me."

"You're welcome." Grace placed her hand on the table, and Chase slipped his into hers. "I have an idea, and don't be angry, but it's shop talk."

"Go ahead."

"It's so beautiful here, I'd like to take your picture." Grace winked. "I'll send it to you. First one for your new phone."

"How does taking my picture have anything to do with work?"

"If you don't mind, I'd like to share pictures of our pilot turning lemons into lemonade, enjoying his unexpected layover in Miami Beach. You're not hard on the eyes and people will take notice. We'll shine a good light on what happened. I'll give it the hashtag lemons to lemonade. I already have video evidence it was the seats rattling then showing them unmovable, before and after proof."

"You'll share them on Facebook, Instagram and so on." Chase nodded approval. "Can't hurt."

"You're not mad? Thinking I'm taking advantage?"

It's the reason I'm here, sweetheart, to help the company. "Not mad, and no, you're not taking advantage if I agree."

"Do you mind if I take pictures now, before the sun sets?"

"Sure. We can go out on the beach."

"Won't we lose the table?"

"Nah, I'll make sure we won't."

* * * *

The ocean breeze helped cool the day where temperatures had pushed to over ninety degrees. After the promotion photo shoot, Grace continued taking pictures of herself and Chase. He swung her around at the waist as she recorded the motion, laughing the whole time. When he set her down, his eyes seemed to drink her in, and she didn't move, not wanting to end the moment. Grace gave a slight nod, and he dipped his head, placing his lips on hers, kissing her so tenderly she almost gasped.

"Hungry?" he whispered.

"Oh, yes," she breathed back.

"Let's go up to the table then."

Ugh. He meant food, stupid. Grace felt his hand slid into hers and they walked to the stairs. When they stepped onto the deck, she gestured toward the building. "Restrooms?"

"Yeah, inside. I'll meet you at the table."

Grace walked past a group of jovial young men, realizing one of them was Chase's friend. She took a quick glance toward the table. Nash looked confident and in charge, reminding her of Chase in a way. One extra glance at his abs, and she found the women's restroom.

The place was empty. I would be a quick in and out. But while in the stall, the door opened, and she heard two giggling voices.

"O.M.G., Tracey, he gave you *another* hundred!"

"Yeah, to keep the table, but make it two hundred. I would have saved it anyway. The guy's a big tipper. Don't know why he isn't at Nash's table."

"Isn't it obvious? He's on a date."

"With his *sister*."

They broke into hysterical laughter.

The first voice spoke again. "It's not really his sister, is it?"

"Might as well be. If I was her, I'd be sitting on his lap by now, tongue down his throat."

"Maybe it's a first date."

Grace was beginning to like the first girl, the second not so much. Number One seemed to have more sense. Did she come to gossip with Number Two or use the bathroom? She'd be stuck in the stall all night if they didn't do something soon. And to top it off, she might join them in their next fit of laughter as she realized she referred to them as number one and two … in a bathroom.

"First date or not," the second girl responded. "I'd still be doing the same thing! Or maybe a good lap dance."

They laughed again.

"She's pretty. They make a great couple," the first girl said.

"Better hurry and tell her because next time he comes in, I'm saying I'm available." Grace heard the entrance door pulled back. "Got to get back to my station, the patrons are calling," she said dramatically. "See you out there."

The girl who stayed in the bathroom finally entered a stall. Grace flushed the toilet and made her getaway, keeping her head down. She washed her hands and flew out the door, banging right into a hard body. Her hand grabbed the stranger's solid arm for balance.

"Sorry, Grace," Nash said with a smile. "You came out so fast, I didn't have time to stop."

"It's nice to run into you again," Grace answered, hoping he got the joke as she pushed by him. Panic set in. The woman still in the bathroom might come out and recognize her as Chase's date, realize Grace was in the other stall and heard the women's conversation. Humiliation would ruin the date.

"Good running into you, too." Nash called after her.

"I hope you don't mind that I ordered," Chase said when Grace sat down.

"Not at all. I'm starving." She covered her face. "You probably wondered why I was gone so long."

"Nope, not at all." Chase slowly shook his head, holding back a laugh.

"I couldn't come out of the stall." Grace bit into her bottom lip. "Two women were discussing us."

"You should have confronted them. Which ones?" Chase sat tall scanning the deck.

"It doesn't matter. In my head, I named them Number One and Number Two as I listened."

Chase cracked a smile and shook his head. "Well, that serves them right." He bent down as if he wanted to tell a secret. "I will never look at any of the employees the same again. I'll always wonder if they're One or Two."

Grace thanked him with her eyes as the server placed the food on the table. The evening sky had set upon them and she planned to make the most of it.

* * * *

They walked hand in hand down the hotel hallway to Grace's room. When they reached her door, she turned and leaned against it. "I had a great time, Chase. Thanks."

He brushed her blonde hair from her face and leaned toward her. His mouth moved against hers and she responded in kind. He'd hoped for an invitation to come in after giving her a lustful kiss. Chase pulled back and waited, finally asking, "I guess we fly back tomorrow, skeleton crew?"

"I'll text Paul and get the details. Breakfast?"

Damn, do I have to ask? "Sure, but I was hoping to be…" He pointed at the door.

"Oh! I'm sorry. Come in."

Grace had a suite, bed and sitting area, different from his one king bedroom. "Nice."

"Sorry. The hotel only had two left. I gave the other one to Halle."

Chase strolled to the sofa and sat, watching Grace pull a bottle of wine from a bag on the dresser. *Maybe I'm not giving her enough credit. She had a bottle waiting for us.* "Let me." He got up and walked toward her, now closer to the bed.

Her hand slightly trembled when she gave him the bottle. Chase set it on the dresser, took her in his arms and kissed her as he felt her grip onto his shirt. He caressed her bare arms and slid to her waist. She shivered when he slid his lips down her neck and over to her ear.

Chase carefully laid her on the bed, gazing into her eyes, noticing the desire. He didn't want to lose control, not knowing where the night might lead. Yet, he wanted her not for one night but for many. He'd never felt connected to a woman like he did Grace. When Nash crashed the party earlier, all Chase thought of was Grace, protecting her, not wanting her hurt. *I don't think this is what Mr. Smith had in mind. Oh, the hell with it.*

His mouth crushed against hers, and Chase felt her arms close around him. Grace pulled his polo over his head with ease, and her dress seemed to disappear, leaving her in a matching set of lingerie. The long silver chain dangled between her breasts, and he finally got to examine what hung from it, a locket. He fingered the oval gently in his hand, producing a gasp from Grace. "What?" He whispered, stroking her bare belly. "Did I do something wrong?"

"Yes … no … it's me." Grace scrambled to sit up and pulled her dress over her head. "I'm sorry, Chase, you need to leave." She tossed his polo at him.

"Oh, no, you don't." Chase tugged on his shirt. "I'm staying here until you tell me what this is about. I touch the stupid necklace, and you freak out."

"It's not stupid." Grace hung her head. "If I tell you my story, you'll be the first one to hear it. I told no one. Then knowing you know … if this doesn't work…" She gestured toward him then touched her chest. "I want to trust you, need to trust you."

Chase grasped her hand and kissed it. "You can." Not the evening he imagined, but Chase decided Grace needed to spill her inner demons if they were to be together. "If you want to share, I will listen."

"I'm sorry about this." Grace ran her fingers along the mattress. "I wanted to, Chase, more than you know."

"But I touched the necklace."

"I should have never left it on." Grace popped it open, showing him a picture of a handsome Asian man. "That's Sean."

"Come on, let's sit over there." Chase nodded at the sofa. He opened the wine, poured two glasses and brought them to the table.

Grace turned her head away from Chase when he sat next to her and whispered, "I loved him very much. He was my life, and I pictured being with him forever."

"Where did you meet Sean?" Chase asked.

"College," Grace answered, taking a glass from the table. She inhaled the aroma of the wine as if for courage. "Sean O'Donnell was the sweetest, kindest man I ever met."

O'Donnell? Chase wrinkled his brow but said nothing.

"I recognize the look. Sean's family came from Japan over one hundred years ago. They've been here for three generations. His mother married an Irishman. He always enjoyed the looks he'd get from people when he told them his name. His sense of humor was awesome."

"Sounds like a great guy."

"He was. I started dating him junior year, we were both business majors. He planned to join the family business, and they offered me a position after graduation. I was torn because Dad always thought I'd work at Falcon."

"Either way, you had a job. Good position to be in."

"Yes, it was. The day after we graduated Sean and I drove to Myrtle Beach to celebrate. We stayed until early evening and got a room. Somehow, don't ask me how, we found one, more like a penthouse than hotel room. I wanted to stay up all night and enjoy the view and the wonderful space he found for us. Sean said he'd like to walk on the beach one more time before we settled in for the night."

Chase thought her story sounded romantic and wondered what happened. He kept quiet, not wanting her to stop and poured more wine.

"We walked close to the waves on the wet sand. Sean drew a heart and put our initials in it. We were being silly. He ran ahead, telling me to stay put. I watched him work in the sand until he waved me over." Her eyes filled with tears. "I couldn't believe what I saw. It said, 'Grace, will you marry me?' I had no idea he would ask so soon, and I guess neither did he. It happened spur of the moment."

Chase wanted to ask if she said no and they had a big fight, broke up, and she never saw him again.

"Sean said, 'I don't have a ring!', upset he didn't plan better. I said yes, I'd marry him, ring or no ring. He took me by the arms, told me to go to our room and he'd be right back. I begged him not to leave and stay with me. A ring wasn't important. But by then, Sean had become so determined, he didn't hear me. He walked me to the door of the hotel and disappeared into the parking lot. I called after him, 'Please don't leave me', and I never saw him again … alive, that is."

Grace's head dropped as she wiped the corner her eyes with a finger. "A drunk driver hit him while he ran to his car. The guy never saw him as he sped through the lot."

"Grace," Chase said and took her hand. "I'm so sorry. You're being loyal to Sean and I understand why."

"You do?" Grace lifted her eyes to meet his.

"You feel you'd betray him if you ever loved anyone else."

"Wow, that's deep." The corners of Grace's mouth twitched.

"Thank my sister." Chase rubbed his chin, deciding not to compare their two stories. He'd gone through a teenager's love crisis with his sister. When her first boyfriend moved three states away, she cried and cried. His mom called and asked him to talk to her. Ella finally broke down and told him her feelings. She loved him, and how could she ever love again?

"I will when I meet her."

They sat in comfortable silence, drinking wine until they finished the bottle.

"I can let him go," Grace whispered. "For the right man."

"I'll take that as a compliment." Chase rose from the sofa. "If I don't leave now, we may have a repeat performance of earlier, and I don't think you're ready for that."

"I will be, Chase." Grace stood and placed her body against him, giving him a lingering kiss. "I'll see you in the morning."

CHAPTER SIX

Chase had a restless night. Old memories dogged his sleep. His father haunted his dreams. The old man wore ragged clothes and had his hand out, asking for money. He shook his head as he walked to the elevator. *No one would catch Sam in worn clothes or anything off the rack.* Chase tried to remember his grandmother's saying about his dad. *Was it champagne taste on a beer budget?*

After breakfast, Grace, Halle and Kyle waited for Chase in the lobby. They had eaten earlier, discussed flight details and discovered they had the rest of the day off once back in Charlotte. Chase thought Halle had tried to send telepathic signals to him while they ate but brushed it off as his imagination in overdrive. As he got off the elevator, he saw Halle get up and walk away. He hung back. It was too much of a coincidence.

She walked down another hall leading to the restrooms. Torn if he should follow or not, he took the chance. If Halle disappeared into the ladies' room he'd turn around.

"Thank goodness you got the hint!" Halle startled him as he rounded the corner. "I was starting to think we had no vibe between us. If we fly together, we've got to have it."

Chase grinned. "I thought you were mind melding with me at breakfast … or do you have to…?" He gestured to the women's restroom.

"Get over here." Halle crossed her arms over her chest, leaned against the wall and chuckled. "Look, Chase, this might not be a big deal, but Grace told me Mark will fly the Miami route for the weekend. We'll have a few days off after the so-called scare in the sky. You don't know this, but he wanted this assignment. I was surprised he didn't get it, especially being the owner's son."

Another one to add to the list? Or did Mark do something to the plane to make us look incompetent? "I didn't know he wanted Miami, but my excuse is I started on Monday."

"Very funny. It's Friday so you've been here five days. Get up to speed." Halle dropped her arms. "Seriously, I never trusted Mark. He's out for himself. If he wants something, he goes after it. We may lose this route, and truthfully, I deserve it. I can go home every night. Kyle and I can work on…" She waved her hand. "Oh, never mind."

"A baby." Chase finished for her. "We won't let him win, Halle. We're a team he won't break up."

"Okay, let's get back before we raise suspicions."

"They don't know I'm here yet." Chase enjoyed bantering with Halle but kept a straight face.

Halle nudged his arm. "Come on, flyboy." They walked around the corner to where everyone sat in a group of chairs placed in a circle. "Look who I found coming out of the elevator," Halle said to Kyle and Grace. "He's *finally* here."

"Paul filed the flight plan. I'm waiting for his text," Grace said. She smiled up at Chase. "Seems like we're flying in some high rollers."

"Really?"

"A Nash Gill? Know him?" she teased. "Paul found out someone was looking for a last-minute flight, and he beat out a private airline with his bid."

Great. What is Nash doing? And what was Paul thinking? He's not a private airline. Besides, we have no flight attendants. "What time do we check in?"

Grace looked at her watch. "Eleven. Flight leaves at twelve. We're waiting on two more people then we'll head over."

Sue Ann and Peter rushed up to the group. "We're here!" Sue Ann sang.

"You two didn't fly back?" Chase now understood why Paul made the bid.

"They didn't need us," Peter explained. "Paul said we should stay overnight. It worked out perfectly. You have us for the flight home and Sue Ann got to work on her tan."

"O … kay." Chase widened his eyes, unable to look at Grace. "Glad you had fun. Should we head over?"

"Are you grumbling to yourself?" Grace teased as they walked to the airport.

"No … maybe."

"Funny how Nash ended up on our plane, isn't it?"

Not funny at all. But, if you knew him, he'd think it's hysterical. Probably did it on purpose. He's the prankster of the group.

"Did you say something?" Grace asked.

"Yeah, I said it'll be great to catch up with him." Chase heard laughter when they reached the gate.

"Chase, old buddy." Nash raised a hand in greeting, said something to the three men he sat with, got up and walked toward them. "Hello, again, Grace." He nodded. "Mind if I steal this guy for a minute?"

"For a minute," Grace said with a wink.

"Promise." Nash placed his hand over his heart.

"Let's talk over there," Chase pointed to a row of empty seats, not happy with the flirting between Grace and Nash. "What's up?" he asked when they were alone.

"I got a call from Mr. Smith." Nash wiggled his eyebrows. "Or Charlie, as I like to think of him."

"Charlie?"

"You know, Charlie's Angels? They always talk to him but never see him."

"They were all women!"

"Dude, can't you take a joke. Stop being so serious for a minute."

"You're not the first one on assignment, Nash. It's my ass on the line. If I blow it, I do everyone in. Including you."

Nash lifted one side of his mouth and a shoulder. "Easy come. Easy go."

"You've been living the good life too long. You should never have that attitude."

"Chase, if it weren't for you, I'd own one gym in Miami. You helped me learn about franchising, invested my money and lectured me if I strayed from our goal. You are my number one friend, Chase. Don't tell the others." He chuckled. "You seriously need to lighten up. Grace can't stop checking you out."

"She's probably looking at you, Nash." Chase bumped his friend's solid arm with his fist and rolled his eyes. *How much does he work out to get that way?*

"Nope, she only has eyes for you."

"Let's get back to Mr. Smith's call. I didn't get one. What did he say?"

"He wants me to come to the bunker this Sunday."

The Society called the new building on Chase's property, the bunker. "And the others? Did he summons them?"

"Haven't heard from them. When I saw Falcon on the website for private rentals, I jumped on it, hoping it was you. I'm not trying to mess up what you have going here. I needed to talk to you."

"I know you can't contact me. I only have a burner phone. Remember my name is Chase *Garrett*. I told Grace we're acquaintances from college." Chase looked over at the three guys Nash had brought with him. "Who are they?"

"Finalists for the Charlotte franchise, first Gill's Gym outside of Florida. I'll be in town for a week."

"Use your room at my house." Each of the five billionaires had rooms at their homes for the others in the society.

"Not this time, bro. I made reservations for all four of us at the same hotel. Can't go disappearing on them." Nash shook his head. He looked over his shoulder. "Do you think Mr. Smith is spying on us right now?"

"Maybe?" Chase cringed.

"We might be in big trouble." Nash laughed and poked Chase with his elbow.

"You still have your phone?"

"Yeah, why?"

"I had to turn mine over and use a burner. There's no way we can stay in touch."

"Unless you give me the number or *you* call *me*. Duh." Nash looked at Chase from the corner of his eye.

"Charlie will know."

Nash chuckled. "Hey, were you making a joke?"

"Yeah, but let's not call him Charlie. Stick with Mr. Smith. It might make him angry."

"Can you call him from the burner?"

"Yeah, and I plan to get in touch with him when I get home tonight."

"What do you think my assignment will be?" Nash shook his head. "I admit, I'm a little nervous."

"As you can tell, I'm working for an airline. I can't say what you'll be doing."

"I hope it's something cool. Double-oh-seven shit."

"He won't tell you much when he goes over the details. You guys heard most of my assignment. Our private meeting was to set up day, time, place. When I called him after my first day at Falcon, I said I could easily fix their problems with my money … if I had it. He said, 'Dig deeper'."

"Have you?"

"I have my suspicions why Falcon is losing money this year. It's not because of bad business practices or loss of passengers."

"Hopefully, you'll be at the meeting Sunday. Maybe Mr. Smith wants you to update me on your progress. Fill me in on what it's like going undercover. Hey, this might mean I'm next!" Nash hummed the Mission Impossible theme song.

"Chase?" Grace called to him. "We're boarding."

"This may be the last time we talk, Nash. I wish I could give you more information. Maybe I'll see you Sunday?" He nodded toward the three men gathering their luggage. "Which one is getting the franchise?"

"See the taller black guy?" Nash answered. "He was in the Army, is fighting PTSD and has a great background in business. I'm leaning his way. The other one is a high school P. E. teacher and wants to own a gym. He has no plans to give up his day job and will let his high school students use it for free."

"Hard choice. What about the other guy?"

"He came from Cuba three years old with a great background in working out fighters, started his own gym from nothing down there."

"One new franchise. Three great picks."

"Trouble is, the veteran may get it on logistics alone. He's ready to move anywhere. The gym teacher is from Pennsylvania. He's a football coach, too, and I don't think he really wants to give up his day job or get a new teaching job in Charlotte. He's trying to get his foot in the door, learn about the business. Victor, the guy from Cuba, would really like to stay in Miami. He's trying to get the rest of his family here."

"Good luck." Chase slapped him on the back. "Grace doesn't look too happy with me. I've got to get going."

* * * *

"What are they be talking about? Chase said they're acquaintances from college," Grace tilted her head as she murmured to Halle.

"Looks may be deceiving," Halle answered.

"What does that mean?" Grace tried to give her an angry look but ended up smiling. "You are one of my best friends, Halle, but if you're holding back, you better start talking."

Halle held her hands in the air. "I know nothing!" She laughed. "But, from what I can tell, especially after breakfast, Chase is into you."

"I told him about Sean."

"You did?" Halle looked truly surprised. "He didn't run for the hills after you told him?"

"Go ahead and say it like you always do. I need to take Sean off the pedestal. I gave him a little push last night."

"I'm not saying to stop loving the man, Grace. I'd always love Kyle, too. But, you're young and have so many years ahead of you."

"You sound like my mother or if I ever talked to my mom, she might say that." Grace pressed her lips together, deciding to test her friend. "Although June makes a good replacement."

"That she does." Halle nodded. "She's the mothering type."

Grace stared at her. "You know."

"Know what?"

"My dad and June?"

"Work together?" Halle scrunched her shoulders.

"How long have they been dating?"

"Paul and June are dating? Cool!" Halle made praying hands. "Please don't. Ooh, you're making that pouty face. Stop now! All right. Three months!"

"Now, was that so hard?" Grace smirked.

"Yes, like ripping off a band aid. Let's go. Chase already entered the skywalk." Halle turned to Kyle who was doing something on his phone. "Babe! Come on. Don't want to leave you behind."

Grace had a new outlook and silently thanked Miami for the change of heart. If the plane hadn't had problems, she wouldn't have gone to the beach with Chase, confided her innermost secret and started the healing process. She inhaled and headed down the skywalk. If Chase didn't ask her out this weekend, she planned to invite him to dinner. *After the lunch and dinner dates he took me on, it sounds a little boring. On the flight back, I'll come up with something.*

Chase waited for her at the opening to the plane. "I was hoping to see you this weekend. Do you have any plans?"

Grace swallowed, almost tripping over the step. Her mind had been in the same place and he caught her off guard. "No plans."

"I thought we'd rest tonight, but I'd like to spend the day with you tomorrow."

And night? "I'd love it."

"Are you going to headquarters after we land?" he asked.

"Yes, I need to check in."

"And, so do I," Chase said. "To learn if I still have a job."

"You will." Grace's heart pounded. She'd forgotten about the fight between her dad and Chase, making a mental note to send a text before take-off.

"You sound sure of yourself. I'll take that as a good sign." Chase glanced down the aisle. Nash and his three companions had taken over the seats four rows back and were in deep conversation. He took Grace by the shoulders and stepped back into the skywalk bringing her with him. "I can't resist you."

Grace shuddered with excitement as he drew closer. A light spicy scent filled her nose, and she touched the side of his face, feeling the close trim of his beard. "I may not have told you this, but I love a man with a beard."

His lips found hers before she said another word. Grace lifted her other hand to his face and ran both around the back of his neck and into his hair. Chase pulled her so close, she had to catch her breath.

"I'm ready now," Chase said with a smile.

"Fly us home, Captain," Grace answered with a smile of her own. She fought back the feeling that he could be the one. Close the book on her old life, open a fresh new one. Panic overwhelmed her for a second.

She'd be giving up her well-planned, neat existence. *But that's all you do! Exist. Time for a change, sister.*

* * * *

Chase escorted Grace into the Falcon building. By the time they finished at the airport, had a late lunch with Nash and his three companions, Grace and he barely made it to headquarters by closing time.

"Paul likes to send the employees home at four on Fridays," Grace said. "He'll probably be the only one in the building besides us." She surprised him with a kiss. "I'll text you my address. I may be gone by the time you finish with Dad."

The building had switched to weekend lighting, offices were dark and hallways dim. One room shone brightly, Paul's.

"I'll see you tomorrow afternoon." Chase pointed two fingers her way. "Wish me luck." *Dammit, man! Don't blow this.* He'd rehearsed mea culpas on the way over to turn the blame on himself. Chase stuck his head in the door. "Paul?"

Paul looked up from his paperwork. "Chase, come in and have a seat."

"I'd like to apologize. I jumped to conclusions."

"Maybe you did, but you got me thinking. First, let's finish our conversation from the plane. You appeared to want to say something more before Grace interrupted."

"It's just that…" *How do I say this?* "You told me why you didn't want to raise Grace's suspicions. But the last thing I heard you say was 'Fine, but I can't wait much longer.' Longer for what, Paul?"

Paul shook his head. "Ray knew what I meant, Chase. That's the important part to this puzzle. Is it your business? No. You stuck your nose somewhere it doesn't belong. This is my airline, I run it the way I want, but I have investors now. They are the ones who can't wait to make a profit, get nervous when the stock drops, and I must field calls right and left. It's the reason I couldn't go on the Miami run. I'm trying to cut corners without scaring the kids. This is their legacy. I don't want them to see the old man fail."

"I'd invest." Chase hadn't planned to say the words aloud. "When I save money from the job, that is."

"Not a planner?" Paul folded his hands over his chest and leaned back in his office chair. "Maybe I was wrong about you. You hit me as a solid, sincere guy."

"I was. I am." Chase defended himself. *If only you knew!*

"You still have a job, but you're on probation. Take a few days off and come back on Monday."

"What about the Miami route? I was supposed to take the Sunday flight."

"We have more than one pilot for routes, but I don't have to tell you that. For now, I'm giving Mark your spot. When you come back on Monday, I'll give you your new schedule."

"Mark?" *Halle was right. Damn! I liked that route. Do I take him off the list since he got his way?*

"My son. I'm sure you met him."

Chase nodded. "What about Halle?"

"She'll be his copilot."

"Oh." Chase felt a blow to the stomach. He liked Halle and wanted to fly with her. "She's great."

"Yes, she is. In a few years, she'll be the captain, if she wants."

"Then we're cool?"

"Cool as can be." Paul closed one eye. "I said you got me thinking."

"I remember."

"Do you really think someone wants to sabotage my airline? Not me." Paul held up his hands. "But, someone."

"Maybe." Chase took a breath, not wanting to reveal what Grace confided in him about the books. "From what I've seen since I've been here, you should be doing well. Planes are full. Business is good. I'm an outsider looking in, giving you an observation. What about Ray? I heard he's the best, then the seats are loose. It doesn't add up."

"You don't think Ray's on someone's payroll?" Paul lifted a brow, tapping his finger against his lips. "I find it hard to believe."

"I don't." Chase remembered how the man looked at Grace. He'd never hurt her dad's airline.

"Nothing's one hundred percent but thanks for your insight."

"If that's all, I'll report to you on Monday." Chase hoped he'd find Grace in her office. One more kiss and breathing in her magnolia scent would hold him until her saw her again.

"We're done here."

Chase felt he was being dismissed from the principal's office. He took his time getting up, not to seem too anxious. Once outside in the hall, he turned the corner toward her workspace and picked up speed. From a distance, the room seemed dim. *She may be using her desk lamp.* He skidded to a stop in front of her doorway. "Grace?"

Startled, Chase blinked, and his jaw dropped. Grace wasn't behind her desk. Instead, her brother Tim sat in her place.

CHAPTER SEVEN

Tim looked up from the computer. "Chase! I thought no one was here." The smile on his face did not reach his eyes. Chase had seen the look many times before. "Come in. What can I do to help you?"

"I was looking for Grace." Chase paused. "Do you usually come in after hours to use her computer?"

"Not often, but I don't need to defend myself to you." Tim's demeanor changed quickly to defense.

"I'm sure she has a password. How'd you get in?"

"We share."

Chase didn't quite believe him. "Okay, so what's so important you couldn't wait to talk to Grace and need to break into her computer instead."

"You know what? You don't look like Paul and you don't sound like him. I only answer to him. But, if it will get you off my back, I'm trying to find if Grace put in a pay raise for me. I want to take good news home to my wife. She's not feeling well."

"I'm sorry to hear. Will she be all right?" Chase baited him, knowing Tim's wife was pregnant.

"Yeah, she's pregnant, and it's been stressful. We find out if it's a boy or girl tonight. I wasn't there today when she went for her check-up, and they gave her a sealed envelope after the ultrasound."

"Boy or girl?" Chase asked. "What are you hoping for?"

"What?" Tim gave him a strange look. "Oh, I thought someone told you we already have three girls."

"Mark mentioned it in passing." Chase waited. Many men wanted a son. He'd want a healthy baby. The way Tim answered his question may help keep him on the list of suspects.

Tim hung his head. "I hate to say it aloud. Boy."

"A raise would help with four kids," Chase said, seething inside. "I hope you get your wish." He nodded and turned to go.

"Wait a minute, Chase," Tim called.

"Yes?"

"Do me a favor and don't tell Grace I was in here?"

"Did you find what you wanted?"

"Sadly, no." Tim shook his head and looked at Chase with pleading eyes.

"Will Grace and Paul be at your house tonight for the big reveal?" Chase's curiosity got the best of him, and if Grace attended, she'd tell him girl or boy tomorrow. He also hoped Tim never noticed he avoided answering the question.

"Yes, and Mark, too."

"Good luck then." Chase longed to get to the Honda and drive home. He had his own agenda. *Call Mr. Smith.*

Chase put in an order for a pizza from his phone, started the car and headed for home. After parking the Honda, he walked to the elevator, finding Darcy leaning wearily against the wall.

"Hey, Darcy."

"Perfect." She barely got the word out.

"You okay?" Chase noticed she'd cut her hair to shoulder length, and instead of a red rinse her hair had a tint of lavender.

"Just tired. I did a double shift at the diner and I need to get to the Swan in an hour."

Chase checked his watch. *Seven.* "I ordered a pizza. Why don't you come with me, lay on the couch and I'll do all the prep?"

"What kind?" Darcy lifted her eyes to meet his.

"Pepperoni, mushroom."

"Deal. I can pick off the pepperoni."

"I'll even do it for you," Chase said as the elevator doors slid back.

When they reached his floor, Chase felt so bad for Darcy he wanted to carry her to his apartment.

"I need to shower before work." She stared at him with large brown eyes, and he noticed dark circles under them.

"Why do you work so hard?" Chase unlocked his door, took Darcy by the arm and marched her to his bathroom. "There are clean towels under the sink. Pizza won't be here for a half hour."

"Thanks, Perfect." Darcy kissed his cheek.

Chase thought she smelled like she'd been at the diner all day, a mixture of sweat, cooking grease and food. "Take your time." In the kitchen he found two paper plates, napkins and cups to set the table. "I know there's a dishwasher, but this is easier," he said as he placed them down.

Fifteen minutes later, his buzzer rang. He rushed to the intercom, pressed it and said, "Come on up." Chase walked to the bathroom and tapped on the door. "They're a little early, but pizza's here."

The expected knock came at the door and Chase fumbled in his pocket for cash as he opened the door. "Please set it…" He swallowed hard. "Grace?"

"Surprise?" Grace lifted her shoulders. "I checked your address on your resume. I hope it's okay."

"I'm totally surprised."

"I saw your apartment was on the way to my brother Tim's. They're having a reveal party tonight, and I wanted to shop for the baby tomorrow, if you don't mind." Grace lowered her head. "Lame excuse to stop by, isn't it?"

"No, not at all." Chase heard the shower turn off and prayed Darcy wouldn't appear.

"I wanted to see where you lived." Grace lifted a shoulder. "It's nice."

"If someone would clean around here." Chase nervously chuckled, realizing he'd set the table for two and moved to block her vision.

"I guess I should be going." Grace stepped toward him, placed her hand on his face but her eyes darted in another direction.

"Perfect, is the pizza here?" Darcy called.

When he turned, he saw her wrapped in a towel, wet hair falling around her shoulders. "No, Darcy, not yet."

"Got a hair dryer?"

"Yeah, look around." He flinched as he turned back to Grace. "It's not what you think." *Now who sounds lame.*

"Oh, it's exactly how it looks." Grace trembled. Her mouth quivered. "I'm sorry I bothered you. I'll see you at work Monday."

Chase gripped her arm. "You're not leaving yet." He pulled her into an embrace, worthy of a swoon-inducing movie hold. "I just found you, and you're not leaving me."

"I am, and I will." Grace shrugged him off.

"It's my friend, Darcy. She worked a double shift at a diner today. I ordered a pizza and offered to share. Would I be telling you this if I was trying to cover something up?"

"Yes … no … I don't know." Tears filled her eyes.

Chase tugged her to him, kissed her lips as if he'd never be with her again. "Text me your address if you want me to come over tomorrow." He walked with her to the door. "I just got home. She smelled to high heaven and has to go to her other job."

"Other job? The girl from the bar?"

"Yeah, that one." Chase heard the buzzer and reached over to answer the intercom. "Yes?"

"Pizza."

"Bring it up to five-twenty," Chase answered, aware that Grace was still there. "I'll wait for your text."

The elevator doors opened, and Grace and the pizza kid passed by each other in the hall. Chase paid, put the food on the table and waited for Darcy.

"Woman troubles?" Darcy strolled down the short hall from the bathroom wearing one of his white t-shirts with her jeans. "You got damn good products in there. Although." She crossed her arms. "It makes sense. Look at you. Perfect."

"Sit. Eat."

After they finished, Chase made Darcy lay on the couch while he cleaned up. He came and sat across from her, fresh from a shower, thinking she looked like a kid. A brotherly feeling of protection overwhelmed him while he studied her relaxing on the sofa. She was a year older than his sister, Ella, and at one time that wouldn't make a difference. Chase would make his moves, keep the girl in his life for a few months then break things off. Instead, his heart broke thinking of Ella working doubles and going to another job in the evening like Darcy had to do. *What's happening to me?*

"Talk to me, Perfect. I don't want to fall asleep. I need to leave soon."

"How about if you talk? Tell me about yourself. Did you go to college? Why do you work two jobs?"

"Did you really ask those questions? Boring." Darcy scoffed. "No to college, although I'd love to go. I always wanted to, but we didn't have enough money. It's just mom and me. No dad ever. Mom's always worked two jobs. I'm following the family tradition."

"Where does your mom work?"

"The diner. She does doubles most days. Mom started a college fund for me when I was in high school. There might be enough by the time I'm forty."

Chase shifted in his seat. "Are you saving?"

"I add to it when I can, but I refuse to live with my mommy at twenty-three. Most of what I make goes to cost of living. I'm a hamster in one of those spinning wheels." Darcy had been staring at the ceiling and now turned toward him. "You know?"

"I think I do."

"You don't. You're a pilot. They make good money, right?"

"It's not a bad living."

"Then why live here? You make enough money to move on up."

"I recently moved here and looked for a place close to work."

"Oh." Darcy seemed lost in thought. "Was that your girlfriend? She's a looker."

"Not really. I'm hoping though."

"Well, snap her up before someone else does. Hell, I'd even take a shot at her." Darcy laughed, then grew serious. "I hope I didn't ruin anything you had going with her."

"Let's say it shocked her to see you. If she didn't accept the truth, then maybe we weren't meant for each other."

"Well said, Perfect." Darcy sat up and ran her hand through her now dry hair. "I should go downstairs and change." She tugged on the shirt. "I'll get this back to you."

"Don't work too hard," Chase called after her, feeling a twinge of guilt. "She works too damn hard." He dug for the burner in his back pocket. The day had gone from good to bad. How much worse could it get? Chase dialed and waited.

"Mr. Young."

It felt odd to hear his real name after saying Chase Garrett all week. "Mr. Smith." He paused. *You speak, you bastard.*

"How was your day?"

"You know how it was."

"Mr. Gill is persistent, isn't he?"

"He's in North Carolina, if that's what you mean."

"I asked him to stay after he settles his business affairs."

"Is he next?"

"We will have to wait until Sunday to find out."

Chase squeezed his free hand into a fist. "Will we? Why don't you be straight with me and tell me what's happening? Are the others going to be there? Am I invited? Do I get to finish this assignment before you're doling out the next one? Damn!"

"You think you had a bad day, Mr. Young. You have not, you made progress."

"Did I now? Why don't you tell me what progress and answer my god-blessed questions?" But no matter how angry he got, Mr. Smith's tone remained the same, making him even more angry.

"Something isn't right at Falcon and I assume you started your list of suspects."

Chase took a deep breath. "Yes." He told the names and reasons he suspected them.

"Very good."

"One more thing before we go," Chase said. "Darcy, shit, I don't know her last name, lives in my building. Even if I don't get my money back, I want an anonymous scholarship given to her from a local college. Promise that now."

"Darcy, shit, I don't know her last name will get a scholarship," Mr. Smith answered.

"Well, look at you. You *do* have a sense of humor."

"And now I have a request."

"Okay, fair is fair."

"Do not put Ms. Edison on your list of suspects. She may appear fragile and willing to do anything to save the company, but Grace is a strong woman of character."

"I won't. And I haven't. By the way, Mr. Smith, how do you know Grace Edison? Mr. Smith, are you there? Mr. Smith?"

* * * *

The next morning, Grace paced through the rooms in her condo. *Send a text. Don't send a text.* "Chase seemed believable. But he never explained who I was to the girl who came out of the bathroom wrapped in a towel. A towel!" She ran her hand through her hair and tugged. "Ooh! What do I do?" She stared down at her handbag she'd dropped in the middle of the living area floor last night. Emotionally exhausted, Grace had gone straight to bed. "Shop!"

Her brother's baby reveal party had inspired her to drive to a boutique and buy out the place. Grace walked through her kitchen to the garage, got in her car and made it in record time. She checked her watch. "Ten-fifteen, they should be open."

Grasping the steering wheel, she stared at the store. "Babies," she whispered and let out a long breath. She grabbed her phone, pulled up Chase's number and texted him the store address along with 'Meet me here.'

"It's a start." She sat in the car a few minutes. "This was a dumb idea. I can't wait here for him. What if he doesn't come?"

Grace hopped from the driver's seat and took notice of the glorious day, blue skies and sunshine. She strolled to the shop, looking in the windows, pretending to be interested. By her calculations it would take Chase fifteen minutes if he was ready. She'd already wasted five. The boutique was nestled among a group of stores, so she walked down the street, checking them out. Satisfied ten minutes had gone by, she walked back to the baby shop.

"Hello!" a middle-aged woman called to her. "Can I be of help?"

"Not yet, but soon," Grace answered. "I want to browse first."

"Enjoy, I'll be here if you need me."

They'd divided the store into infant and toddler girl, boy and neutral clothing and accessories. She strolled around the tables until she heard the front doorbell and her heart skipped a beat. When Grace glanced toward the entrance, she saw Chase gazing at her. She lifted her hand in greeting.

"I'm glad you texted," Chase said when he reached her. "Although." He looked around and chuckled. "I don't think you live here."

"You're quite the detective, Mr. Garrett." Grace took his hand. "I'm sorry about last night. I shouldn't have surprised you. What you do on your own time is none of my business."

"What I do on my time *is* your business, Grace. Don't you get it? I'm in for the long haul."

Grace studied his handsome face, taking in his features. Dark, smoldering eyes, yet there was a twinkle in them. The well-kept beard and hair showed his personality, how he liked things neat and organized. *Or maybe not, I saw his apartment.* "I am, too, if you can find it in your heart to forgive me."

"There's nothing to forgive." Chase squeezed her hand. "Now, don't keep me in suspense. Boy or girl?"

"Boy. I plan to buy the store out and delivered to Tim's house as a surprise."

"Do you mind if I chip in? My name doesn't need to go on the card. Too soon."

"Agree, too soon." Grace smiled. "I'd love your help."

Once they picked blues and neutrals in every size up to eighteen months, Grace blew a strand of hair from her face. "We're done here."

The store clerk took over, wrapping and packaging the gifts. She thanked Grace many times for her purchase.

"She's a generous woman," Chase said, slipping Grace a few hundred dollars.

She held the bills in the air. "Lunch on me."

They slipped out into the sunny day which had grown warmer in the hour they'd been in the store.

"There's a great bistro down the street," Grace said. "Is that okay?" She recalled the oceanfront restaurant in Miami Beach and knew Chase had good taste when it came to food. "The menu's eclectic. Something for everyone."

"Sounds great."

The hostess seated the couple at an umbrella table on the restaurant's back porch.

"It's too early to eat lunch yet. I'll order a cup of coffee," Grace said to the waitress when she approached.

"I'll have the same," Chase replied. He looked at Grace like he wanted to tell her something yet hesitated.

"What is it?"

"I want to ask you a couple questions and hope you'll answer without asking why. Can you do it?" Chase grimaced.

"I need to hear the questions." Grace's heart pounded. *He wants to know if it's okay if he dates me and Darcy. Argh! Or if I slept with anyone other than Sean. The answer is no!*

"Are you giving Tim a raise?"

"What? Oh, I get it. The baby is another mouth to feed." Grace dabbed her mouth with the linen napkin on her lap. She leaned back as the waitress arrived to pour coffee, giving her time to compose herself.

"I heard he asked, that's all."

"He'll get the raise when I'm ready." Grace chuckled. "I've been preoccupied with other things since he asked. Rattling seats, hashtag—scare in the air."

Chase stirred his coffee, looking thoughtful. "Do you share computers at work?"

"I need more information."

"Let's say Paul's not in the office. You need something that's only on his computer. Do you go in there, sit down and find it?"

"No. We all get passcodes. We agreed if family works together we can't abuse privileges. If Paul wasn't my dad, do you think I'd have access to the owner's computer? Nope." Grace shook her head then stared at Chase. "What happened? You were still at headquarters when I left yesterday."

"Nothing."

Grace sipped from her mug and an idea struck. "Just answer yes or no, Chase. You made a promise not to tell me."

"Not really."

Grace gave him a hard stare.

"All right! No, I made no such promise. Happy?" The corners of his mouth twitched, making Grace want to jump from her seat and plant a kiss on them.

"Was Tim in my office?"

"Yes."

"Damn!" Grace made a fist. "He was trying to break into my computer to find out if he got a raise. I should make him wait longer."

"Does he have money problems?" Chase asked.

"I don't think so." Grace placed her hand on her chin. "If he did, I hope he'd tell us or at least Dad."

"I'm sure he's worked his way up the pay ladder from the starting salary of 90K." Chase raised a brow and smirked.

"Truthfully? I never thought you'd take it, but you did, thank you."

"You're welcome." Chase gave her a smile that made her heart flip. "Before we order lunch, I'd like to talk to you about Darcy."

Grace's stomach dropped. *Oh, no. Here it comes.*

CHAPTER EIGHT

The look on her face killed him. Chase quickly got to the point. "Darcy's a friend, Grace. I want you to get to know her. She's a good kid, working two jobs. Darcy's at the age where she should've finished college and ready to start her life. Instead, she's working to make enough to live day to day. Not a great existence."

Grace's face relaxed, and she wore a look of sympathy. "You told me you had a sister. Is Darcy around her age?"

"Yeah, it got me thinking about Ella. What if she worked a double shift at a diner and had to hurry home, shower and change to get ready for the next job?"

"That's a hard schedule, but lots of people do it. I give them credit."

"I do, too. There's something about Darcy. You'll meet her tonight."

"Tonight?"

"I'm taking you to the Golden Swan for drinks after dinner. I checked, and she's working."

"I don't know if it will help, but I'll go in on a big tip for her."

Chase held back. He wanted to tell Grace about the college scholarship he requested. "She won't take it. Darcy will think it's a sympathy tip."

"Okay, then we'll figure something out. I want to meet her, Chase." Grace pressed her lips together. "Why does she call you, Perfect?"

Leave out the Tiger part. "She thinks I worry too much about how I look." Chase touched his beard.

"I love it," Grace said. "Don't stop."

Chase gestured to their waitress. "We're ready to order now."

As they ate lunch, Chase felt Grace had relaxed. He could sit at the table with her all day, chatting and occasionally ordering food, if it kept her stress-free.

"Do you have swim trunks?" Grace asked.

"Not on me." Chase teased.

"Well, you're going home to get them. I'll text you my address. My condo came with a beautiful pool area and the day is growing hotter by the minute. I thought we'd go for a swim."

Chase swallowed hard. *You in a swimsuit? Hell, yeah.* "I'll get the check."

They parted ways at the baby store's parking lot. Chase pushed the Honda to its limits. He caught the elevator as it hit parking garage level and rushed down his hall to his apartment when the doors opened to the fifth floor. His Falcon bag sat in a corner of the bedroom and he threw a few things in besides a swimsuit. The burner phone vibrated, and he checked the screen for the address. "Got it."

Grace's condo development appeared new, well-landscaped and tastefully decorated. "Finn would approve." Chase leaned his head against the seat as he took in the surroundings. "Maybe he'll be there on Sunday?"

Finn, the only privileged one in the Society, was his college roommate. He came from a family of long-time real estate investors. They owned hotels, vacation rentals and built upscale housing divisions. Their list of holdings was long and solid. Finn may have been rich, but he wanted to find his own way. When the six of them discussed the Secret Billionaire Society as a joke, Finn was first onboard. *When did it turn serious?*

Chase hadn't received orders from Mr. Smith and wondered if he was invited to the Society meeting.

"Good thing I'm on probation or I couldn't go if I *am* summoned. They'd scheduled me to fly the Miami route tomorrow," he mumbled to himself. He checked his phone once more, looked at Grace's address to make sure he had the right place and hopped from the car.

Grace answered the door in a two-piece suit with a sarong tied around her waist. "You made it." She stepped back. "Come in."

Chase followed her to the kitchen. Grace had covered plates of cheese and crackers with plastic wrap. She picked them up and placed the food in a cooler. "There's a bottle of wine in the fridge. Would you mind?"

"Sure." He found a bottle of red and handed to her.

"Oh, I almost forgot! The grapes."

"Got 'em." Chase took the zipped bag from a shelf. "You come prepared."

"Always do. The pool's not far, but I don't want to come back if I don't need to."

Once through the pool's security gate, Chase felt he'd left North Carolina and walked into the tropics. A huge kidney-shaped pool with water falling over levels of shale and rock at the deep end was the focal point. Large palm trees surrounded the area with one placed right in the pool inside a container garden. He whistled. "Nice."

"This sold me on the condo. I fell in love with this." Grace pointed to the pool.

Lounge chairs and chaises were discreetly set around the slate-stone deck. Carefully placed mini gardens filled in the gaps.

"Pick a spot," Grace said, lifting her sunglasses to gaze at Chase.

"Somewhere secluded. I don't want any nosey neighbors ogling us, wondering who you brought to the pool," he teased.

Grace giggled. "I only know a few people in the development. Sad thing, not too many use the pool. It's an adults-only condo association. People are busy, I guess."

Chase had noticed the lack of children. Studying the pool, he saw no slides or play equipment. *Definitely not kid friendly.* "I, for one, am glad you brought me here." He spotted two chaises with a table between them. "How about there?"

They set up the drinks and food, sitting across from each other while they ate. Grace stood, took her plastic wine glass and offered her hand, "Let's go sit in the shallow end."

Chase willingly followed, checking the deck for people. "Is no one here?"

"There will be later this afternoon and into the evening. I hoped it'd be like this." Grace stepped smoothly into the water and down the three stairs, over to the edge. She leaned against the wall and placed her wine on the cement stone behind her.

Chase walked up to her, slipping his arms around her waist. To him, she was an angel.

"I'm sure you've been with many women," Grace said, fluttering her eyes. "I'm just…" She glanced down at her bathing suit top. "Average."

"Never say you're average. You're beautiful, Grace." Chase found her lips, tasting the dry red wine. "In fact, if we weren't in this pool…"

"Come on." She took his hand and pulled him farther into the water. Grace swam toward the waterfall. "It's deeper there, but you can still stand."

Chase prided himself on being a good swimmer. He did laps daily in his long, rectangle pool outside his bedroom, especially made for him. He knew how many strokes from one end to the other. The second pool, located in the backyard, had been designed with both kids and adults in mind. Not too many children used the slide coming out from the edge of the waterfall, but his friends loved it.

"What are you thinking about, Chase?" Grace asked. "Sometimes it seems you're in another place."

"No." He shook the water from his ears as he found the bottom. "I'm right where I want to be." Even in the water, he felt the heat from her body. If he didn't back away now, he'd take her right in the pool. *With her permission.*

"Where are you going?" Grace draped an arm over each of his shoulders.

"I … um…"

"Want me?"

He didn't know if it was the afternoon wine, but Chase wanted to be careful. "Yes."

"We're the only ones here." Grace teased.

"I don't think you want me to ruin your reputation in your home pool." Chase lifted his brows.

Grace swam toward him, wrapped her legs around his waist and kissed him. She slid over to his ear and whispered, "What if I do?"

She's not making this easy! Chase pulled her body closer and floated backward to the deepest end of the pool. From the corner of his eye, he saw he could turn a corner and float into the farthest end, away from the entrance. Grace's eyes were closed, and she let Chase guide her to the spot. *Okay, baby, our first time will be in a pool.* He had to smile.

"You're sure about this," he whispered in her ear.

Eyes still closed, Grace nodded as she found his lips.

* * * *

"I hope you don't mind leftovers," Grace said over her shoulder. She hummed as she grabbed leftover lasagna from the fridge. Her mind spun with the excitement of having pool sex. It had been mind-blowing and terrorizing rolled into one. Once her head cleared from the wine, she was happy no neighbors had come to the pool. At the time, she didn't care. *Let them see me*, her mind had screamed. Good girl Grace having sex in the pool with a guy she's known for five days.

Afterward, she and Chase dozed on the chaises, packed away the leftovers and came back to the condo. He offered dinner. She suggested leftovers. They showered together and now he dressed in her bedroom. A shudder went through her. She hadn't felt this alive since … Grace shook her head. *Don't compare.* She turned on the stove, made a salad and chuckled as she worked. *Maybe Darcy is right. Perfect takes a while getting ready.*

Hands slipped around her waist and lips were on her neck. "Can I help?" Chase asked.

"Nope, almost done." She turned her head for a kiss, taking in his fresh scent.

"Smells good."

"We're still going to the Golden Swan?" Grace asked.

"Yes, if you want. Darcy doesn't know we're coming."

Grace picked up the salad bowl, brought it to the table and noticed Chase studying his phone. "Everything okay?"

"What?" He looked up in surprise. "Oh, this?" Chase held up his phone. "An old friend is in town and wants to meet up tomorrow."

"Oh." Grace dropped her shoulders.

In three strides, he stood next to her. "It won't be all day. The meeting's at one. How about I stay the night, we enjoy breakfast together and I'll leave from here?"

"I'd love that," Grace answered.

"Stop doubting me, Grace. Long haul, remember?"

"I'll try. You seem too good to be true."

Chase let out a hearty laugh. "Not at all, baby. You're the one that's changing me." He scratched at the side of his beard, causing Grace to pause.

"You don't have to be in for the long haul, Chase, or change for me," she said to ease his mind. "Wherever this goes, you brought me back into the real world."

"Damn!" Chase dropped his hand from his face and appeared to be angry. "Was I doing that thing to my face again? It's an old habit, something I do it when I get nervous."

"Hmm, giving secrets away?"

"I don't want any between us, but it may take time to tell them all."

The timer buzzed, and Grace grabbed oven mitts. "Sit. I'll bring the lasagna to the table."

"I'll grab the salad."

* * * *

The heat of the day had broken when they stepped out the condo door. The sun had begun to set, and a breeze added to the perfect evening.

"When does Darcy start work?" Grace asked, checking the time. It was almost nine p.m.

"Eight on weekends, seven during the week."

Chase seemed to know a lot about the girl, but Grace held back comment. She wanted to get to know Darcy, Chase's only friend in the city. *Well, Nash is here, but lives in Miami. Then there's the mysterious guy from the text.*

"Now *you* seem far away," Chase said, and touched her cheek with the back of his finger.

"You said you had no friends here, but now you have three."

"Yeah, I make friends easily." He chuckled and pulled into the parking lot behind the rows of bars, shops and restaurants.

"I've never been here," Grace said, looking one way then the other when they reached the street. "It's quaint and beautiful. You live a few blocks away, right?"

"Up this street." Chase pointed to the main one they walked along. "Make a right four blocks down." He opened the door of the Golden Swan for Grace, letting her pass by him.

Music and chatter came from the place, and Chase searched for the band. If they were going to speak with Darcy, he wanted to be heard. He caught the hostess. "Live band?"

"Yes, on the patio. Would you like to sit there?" She held up menus.

"No, we'll sit at the bar."

Darcy hadn't seen them come in and Chase guided Grace to her section of the bar. Her eyes lit up when she saw him. "Perfect!" She lifted her hand. "And Beauty."

Grace slipped onto the barstool and whispered to Chase, "Darcy gave me a nickname. She must like me."

"She must. Would you like a glass of wine?" Chase asked.

Grace placed her hand on her forehead. "I had enough for one day. A beer is fine."

"A woman after my own heart." Chase held up two fingers. "Any good beer on tap, Darcy."

Darcy gave him a nod. Within a minute, she slid two mugs along the bar toward them. "On the house, Perfect."

"Oh, no." Chase shook his head. "See what I mean," he said under his breath to Grace.

Darcy plopped down on two folded arms on the bar in front of them. "You've got the 'I just had great sex look' on your faces. What's going on with you two?"

"You get right to the point, don't you?" Grace laughed. "Maybe we did." She lifted a shoulder, and it was Darcy's turn to giggle.

"Did he tell you what I said?" Darcy pointed at Chase.

"Darcy, no." Chase held up his hands.

"Too soon?" Darcy made a face, teasing him.

"Try like never." He smirked.

"Now, I have to know!" Grace smiled.

"I said," Darcy spoke quietly. "If he wasn't interested in you, I was."

"In me?" Grace placed her hand on her chest.

"Yes, you." Darcy winked.

"You play for both teams." Grace nodded.

"You get it." Darcy cocked her head at Chase. "Him, not so much."

"I like her, Chase." Grace nudged him. "I can see why you two are friends. Darcy might teach you a thing or two." She looked at Darcy and they laughed.

"Okay, stop ganging up on me." Chase grinned. Grace and Darcy appeared to click which made him happy. They may end up being in his life for a long time.

* * * *

Chase woke before Grace and checked the time. *Ten!* He hopped from the bed, quickly showered and dressed. When he came out of the bathroom, he tiptoed to the bed. Grace slept so peacefully, he hated to wake her. He sat on the edge of the bed and stroked her arm. "Grace, wake up. I'll make us breakfast." *One thing I'm capable of doing well.*

"Mmm." She rolled toward him. "I was having the best dream. A handsome man was in my bed making love to me." Grace opened her eyes. "Oh! You're not a dream."

"No, baby, I'm not. But I have an appointment, and I promised you breakfast."

"You're dressed and ready to leave," she pouted.

Chase rubbed her side and around to her bottom, giving it a pat. "You don't need to get dressed yet. Come out and keep me company."

"Okay." Grace popped up, wearing a pink tank and white short shorts, and Chase pulled her onto his lap for a quick snuggle. "If you keep that up," she said. "You'll never get to your meeting."

"It's very tempting." Chase wanted so badly to tell her about Mr. Smith and the guys, but the Society came first. They'd taken an oath. He made a mental note to find out if they could tell a significant other when it was over. *Significant other? We were players. Girlfriends, yes. Long term, no. None of us.*

Grace wrapped her hand under his chin. "Chase?"

"I was preparing the breakfast menu in my head," he answered.

"Right." Grace rolled her eyes and slid from his lap.

"Hey!" Chase caught up to her and nibbled her neck. "See? I'm hungry. Omelets and toast, coming up."

While he worked in the kitchen, Grace showered and got ready for the day. It gave him time to think. *Is Mr. Smith fast tracking the project? Did he discover important information we need to know?* He flipped the omelet, waited a minute and slid it onto a plate.

"Wow, you're good at everything," Grace said, filling her coffee cup.

Chase nuzzled up behind her. "Wish I could stay." He finished his omelet and joined her at the kitchen bar. "If something comes up, I'll text."

"No worries."

A sudden urge to visit home swept over him. Chase missed his two golden retrievers, Belle and Bear, and wanted to see them. He knew the staff cared for them and never worried when he was away on business. "More coffee," he asked, trying not to appear ready to leave.

"I'm good, Chase. I have errands to run and I need to check in at Falcon. Mark's flying to Miami today."

Chase grimaced, surprised by the sting of the comment. "He'll do fine, I'm sure." He wiped his mouth, cleaned up the dishes and kissed Grace on the cheek.

"You can do better than that." She swiveled on the barstool to face him.

"You bet I can." Chase laughed, giving her a solid kiss and headed for the door.

CHAPTER NINE

Chase drove down the winding driveway to his palatial home. The yard looked freshly manicured, and someone had recently swept the drive clean of debris. Too extravagant for one person as his sister Ella reminded him. "At least fill it with a wife and children," she had said. Only one person in his family didn't know where he lived and never would. *The Gambler.*

His favorite part of the house was the outdoor living area, starting with a sunroom and stepping out onto a multi-color stone patio surrounded by large craggy tan rocks in a dry bed setting. Chase had the built-in gas grill, a smoker and refrigerator strategically placed around the edges. His outdoor furniture and table accommodated seating for twelve, the Society plus a guest. From there, a walkway weaved to the pool, changing rooms and bathroom. To the right, tennis courts, and to the left, behind a mass of foliage, his personal lap pool and entrance to his bedroom.

Chase checked the parking spaces next to the garage before he pulled the Honda into the four-car building connected to the side of the house. "I'm the first one here."

His three cars, lined in a row, were cleaned and polished. "Makes you look like you need some work." Chase slipped from behind the driver's seat, slammed the door and patted the blue hood of the Honda. The Aston Martin, Lexus SUV and the practical Audi sedan purchased for his mom and sister's use had been all ordered in black, his preferred color.

Chase heard the dogs barking and knew they waited behind the door. He took one more look out at the extra parking spaces. "For all I know, it could be

Nash and me." The door swung open, and the dogs flew at him.

"Sorry, Chase," his house manager said with a shrug. "They looked so sad."

"I missed them, too, Renata." Chase stepped inside and kissed her cheek. "But I know they're in good hands when I'm gone."

"Your children are my children." She teased. Chase had hired Renata after he built the house five years ago. She was fifty then, always acting more like a mother to the twenty-five-year-old billionaire than someone he hired to run his household.

"Have any of my friends stopped by?"

"You mean the five guys that hang out here more often than you do?" She placed her hands on her hips and chuckled. "Nash was here yesterday. Said he'd be back today."

"Anyone else?"

"Something going to happen in that man cave you built?" she asked, arching a brow. "And while we're on the subject, the staff can clean the outer room, but the door is always locked to the other."

"I told you don't worry about it."

"Okay, but I'm sure it could use a good vacuum and dust. I can have someone in there whenever you give the word."

"Thanks, I'll remember that." Chase smiled. "I'll be in my room."

As he strolled to his bedroom, Chase judged the open space floorplan of his home, trying to see it through Grace's eyes. He liked the one-floor living, although the house had two, and hoped she would, too.

Originally, the hallway to his sanctuary had four bedrooms, two with a connecting bath, and two without. A main bath was at the entrance of the hallway designated for guest use. Chase didn't care which one they used. Nash swore he peed in every toilet in the house. Chase chuckled as he peered into the first redesigned bedroom, his home office. He'd chosen the connecting rooms on the one side of the hall for his workspace. Walking through the bathroom, he came out into his library. Across the hall, he'd left that bedroom, which was closest to his, relatively empty. His mom called it the reading room although it had file drawers along one wall. Chase had chosen a lamp, table and comfortable chair for one corner, and he'd often find her in there with a book. The room next to the reading room, and closest to the hall bathroom, was for his personal secretary, easy access from his office across the hall.

The second story was built expressly for the Society, five separate suites. The basement had a walk-out entrance straight to the pool, and he'd fashioned it as a mini-apartment for his mom, Red and sister.

The dogs trailed him, catching up every so often to glance up with trust and loyalty. When he finished touring the four bedrooms, Chase returned down the hall and into his suite. He sprawled on the bed. Belle and Bear took their places next to it. He'd trained them well, no jumping on furniture, beds or people. He smiled at them, tongues hanging out, panting yet looking serene.

The burner phone vibrated in his back pocket. Chase pulled it and checked the time. *Noon.* It was Mr. Smith or Grace, the only two who had the number. He read a text from Mr. Smith. "Arriving at one o'clock."

"Nash is in the house!" a familiar voice yelled down the hallway. The dogs bounced up, their nails clicking on the hardwood as they scrambled to meet him.

"He's an overgrown child," Chase mumbled, sat up and slid off his bed. He gazed longingly at his lap pool through the French doors, yearning for time to use it.

"I'm the first one here, I guess," Nash said when Chase appeared in the great room.

"We should head over and wait there."

"*They* should be here soon."

"Everyone's coming?"

"I heard from Beau and Finn, so I assumed Kade and Gabe got the message."

"You and I thought you were next, but maybe not." Chase lifted a shoulder.

"Shit, I don't care when I go if I will look the way you do. I swear you've aged five years since we were here last … and that was eight days ago."

"I didn't expect the pressure to get to me."

Nash walked out the sunroom door and turned to Chase. "Besides Gabe, you're the most serious one of the group. That's probably why Charlie picked you first."

"Nash! Dammit, I told you to not use the name. Can you ever be serious?" Chase caught up to him and placed a hand on his shoulder. "Sorry, you're right. I'm the one who needs to lighten up."

"Dude, you were the test subject. I can see why you're wound tight When's the last time you had sex?" Nash pulled open the door to the bunker. Gunshots, loud music and a helicopter sound greeted them. He looked at Chase over his shoulder. "Let the party begin."

Four guys, beers in hand, sat in various spots around the room. One of the *Mission Impossible* movies played on the widescreen, filling up a large part of one wall. The sound dropped when Nash and Chase walked into the room.

"He's still alive, boys!" Finn held up his beer in salute and ran his hand through his blonde hair with the other. "My roomie lives to fight another day!"

"We thought Smith called us here to mourn your demise, Chase." Beau shook his head. "Glad you're still in one piece."

Beau had been Nash's roommate in college, living down the hall from Chase and Finn. Over the years, Nash's laid-back attitude never affected Beau or changed the course he envisioned for himself. He had his sights set on the tech industry, his goal to reach the top ten black billionaires in America and his reason for joining the Society. Nash dragged him along kicking and screaming to the Society, but he became their tech mentor, designing websites, logos and whatever was needed for each member's company. Beau could let loose every so often, some of Nash had rubbed off on him, and now seemed to be one of those times.

"Very funny." Chase smirked. "This isn't as easy as we thought."

The movie and music switched off, and each man sat with their eyes on Chase.

"We want to know everything," Finn said.

"I thought it'd be easy," Chase answered. "Go in. Find the problem. Fix it. Done."

"Not so fast, bro," Nash said, placing his hand on Chase's chest as he made eye contact with the others. "There's a woman, a beautiful, smart, sexy one."

Moans and cheers came from the group.

"We said no women," Gabe called out.

"It just happened." Chase shoved an elbow into Nash's midsection. "Don't listen to him."

"Okay." Gabe nodded." I'm not surprised. The women flock to you. But can you tell us what happened this week?"

Chase tried to sum up the week the best he could—meeting people at Falcon, the problems he found and his suspects.

"It's the dad," Finn said. "The owner can always deflect blame on to others."

"I vote for the brother who has four kids," Kade added.

"The mechanic!" Nash threw out his arms. "He has exclusive access."

"True, unless he's being paid by someone outside of Falcon to sabotage the airline." Beau rubbed his chin. "Falcon stock has been on the rise for the last five years. Once we heard Chase was going there, I did a little research."

"Wait!" Nash held up his hand. "We're forgetting one person. Grace Edison. The owner's daughter and." He cocked his head toward Chase. "His girl."

Chase's temper had been at a slow boil, but now it soared as he grabbed Nash by the shirt. "Shut up, man!" He gave a push and let go. "Mr. Smith said not to put her on the list."

"What?" Nash's eyes were large as saucers. "He knows more than we think."

"Right." Chase nodded. "And for all we know, he's recording this conversation. Whenever I checked in, Smith seems to know the details before I tell him." His phone dinged, and Chase looked at the message. "He's about to arrive. Everyone in the interrogation room."

* * * *

"Nash is next and looked none too happy," Gabe said when the five walked out of the room, leaving Nash behind. "What happens after we leave the room, Chase?"

"Mr. Smith goes over more details, dates, times and people. It's good to hear you guys can keep your phones besides the burner to contact him."

"As someone said before, you were the test subject." Kade clapped him on the shoulder.

"Tiger Eyes" they used to call him in college. His golden-brown eyes and dark looks, shaggy haircut and lean, muscular figure were the perfect characteristics for a male model. He did a few gigs to earn money during and after college but never wanted it as a career. Instead, he wished to be on the other side of the camera, started off doing photo shoots and worked his way through the industry. He now owned a piece of a film studio and a few other holdings, even directed a movie and a few shows for cable. With Chase's help, he'd invested his money wisely.

Nash stormed from the interrogation room, slamming the door behind him. "I don't get to do any double-o stuff! No name change, no Honda, no nothing. What the hell."

"Hard to believe," Chase answered.

"But it makes sense to keep your name, Nash. You *are* the face of your franchise," Kade, who stood next to Chase, replied. "Pretty hard to disguise all this." He waved his hand up and down in front of Nash's toned body.

"Bastard!" Nash grabbed for his hand, but Kade pulled away in time.

While they argued, Chase checked his phone, hoping Grace had sent a message. His heart soared when he saw she had, then it fell as he read, "Called in to office. Don't know how long I'll be. See you tomorrow. Will get back to you on a flight schedule. Talking to Paul later." She placed a pink heart at the end.

A brawl had broken out while he read, but no one would get hurt. They'd done fake choke holds, arms pulled behind backs and takedowns for years. Chase chose not to take part, waited until they paused and clapped his hands. "Time to sit down and listen."

They scrambled for seats and looked up at him. Finn draped his arm over the back of his chair and said, "What is it, fearless leader?"

"I'm not the leader, Finn."

"You are. You just don't know it."

"That's why I like him best," Nash said.

"Hey!" Beau pointed at him. "You always say that to me."

Nash lifted a shoulder and smirked. Others pretended they were hurt, saying they'd heard the same thing.

Chase crossed his arms, stared at the Society and finally said, "Are you guys done?"

Mumblings of "yeah", "go ahead", "Nash is an ass", were heard.

"We are loyal to the Society first," Chase said. "Our holdings may be in a trust, but I still run my private airline. If anyone needs to use it, call Craig. If any of you say it's an emergency, he's to drop everything and get you in the air. As you know, he's run the business with me since the start and on site, with or without me almost twelve hours a day." He shrugged.

"You never know if you'll need to get somewhere in a hurry while on assignment."

"So, don't tell Smith?" Gabe asked, taking off his black frame glasses and wiping them on the edge of his shirt.

"Right and remember this is for emergencies only. When you're not on assignment, it's business as usual. Call the office and make arrangements."

"Can you arrange for me to fly back to Miami?" Nash asked. "I start tomorrow."

"Doing what?" Beau asked.

Nash shrugged. "It's for me to find out," he said and looked at Chase. "He didn't tell Chase much either."

Chase headed for his house phone installed for emergencies. "I'll use this phone. Tell me when you want to leave Nash."

"Tonight."

After Chase hung up, he looked at his group of friends. "If we need each other, call. I don't give a shit what Smith says. It's the six of us with our asses on the line, not him. Our loyalty surpasses any agreement we made."

"Six!" Kade hopped from his seat, holding one arm in the air.

Finn, Nash, Gabe and Beau followed his lead. Chase joined the circle, completing the pyramid they fashioned with their arms, their secret signal, and they shouted, "From the bottom to the top!"

Beau had created a special pyramid to represent them and an emoji for them to use. Sometimes they'd send the pyramid to each other and nothing else. Chase stepped back and rubbed his chin. "Smith doesn't know about the pyramid. Think about it. We might use it to our advantage now we can use our phones."

Chase even had the pyramid incorporated into his private airline logo. Each man had used it in some way, bonding them in ways no one knew.

The day had slipped by and Chase looked at his watch. "Dinner on the patio, everyone."

"Only if Renata made cornbread." Finn teased. "I try to hire her away, but she won't budge."

"We know why," Nash said in a serious tone. "Chase will fly her to visit her daughter any time she wants."

"I could easily hire a jet," Finn answered.

"But, you live in California, Finn. North Carolina is much closer to Florida. Give it up." Nash stood. "As much as I'd like to stay, I'm going to the airport."

Chase shook his hand. "Good luck. I won't be able to reach out until I get my phone back…"

"No worries, bro."

No worries. Hadn't Grace recently said that to him? Maybe it was time the guys grew up. "Yes, worry! I'll be there for you."

* * * *

Grace flipped on her desk lamp, needing more light. She'd left her condo and arrived at Falcon at six-thirty that morning to work on the budget. The quiet, no interruptions helped her think. Her dad would be here soon, but she locked the main door for safety. He'd have her head if he found it opened.

She tapped her lips with a pen. "Perfect time to talk when he gets here. No one's in the office."

By seven-fifteen, she heard footsteps in the hall. When Grace looked up she saw two men, one her dad, the other she didn't recognize, standing outside her doorway.

"If you would be so kind to wait here?" Paul's voice traveled into her office.

Concerned, she rose from her chair when her dad stepped inside and motioned for her to sit. He took the chair in front of her desk.

"What's going on? Grace asked in a stage whisper.

"This guy." Paul pointed with his thumb over his shoulder. "Was waiting in a car outside the building. When he saw me, he got out and I thought he might rob me." His eyes widened. "But, he asked me about a Chase Young, and if he worked here. I invited him in like a fool, but now he seems legit. Do you think Chase Young and Chase Garrett are the same person?"

Grace had been thinking the same thing. "Did he say who *he* was?"

"Sam Young."

The conversation Grace had with Chase came to her. He'd said his dad was a gambler and looked him up when he needed money. *Did Chase change his last name, hoping to be free of Sam?* "Dad." Grace looked at him intently. "Trust me on this. Let me speak with him."

"No, Dumpling. Absolutely not."

"I have more information than you on this situation. If I promise to tell you later, will you go to your office?"

"I'll be in the hall, Gracie. Not more than a few steps away."

"Okay, I can deal with that. When this Sam Young leaves, you and I will discuss Chase." Grace leaned back in her chair. "Send him in."

Grace fought back the shock of seeing Sam Young. A well-dressed man walked into her office wearing a white dress shirt, sleeves rolled to the elbow, black pants tailored to fit his firm body and designer shoes. He appeared to be in his late fifties, dark hair and eyes like Chase without the facial hair. "What can I do to help you, Mr. Young?"

"Sam." He extended his hand. "Pleased to meet you." He glanced around as if looking for her name.

"Grace Edison. Please sit." She waited until he was seated. "Paul tells me you are looking for someone by the name of Chase Young. There's no one on our payroll by that name. Could you tell me why you are looking here for him?"

"He's my son." Sam sat forward, folding his hands. "At times, we're not on good terms. He might work here under an assumed name so I can't find him."

Grace fought to keep a stoic face. "That would be difficult to do in this day and age."

"Okay." Sam lifted a shoulder. "Maybe he went through the legal procedure to change his last name. He has the money to do it."

Money? Now, we're on to the real reason he's here. "I am sorry, Mr. Young. Falcon cannot help you. Paul said you were sitting in your car when he arrived. This is private property. If you continue to do so, we will have you arrested." Grace hoped Chase would be proud of her, defending her man. She pushed back her chair to stand.

"No! Wait." Sam's hands shook when he raised them to stop her. "I want to talk to him, that's all. Will Chase Garrett come to the office today?"

Grace felt torn. Sam looked so sincere, her heart broke. But, if he was a master gambler, he could be playing a part. Yet, was it her decision? "I'll tell you what. You can sit in an unoccupied office at the end of this hall. When Chase arrives, I'll tell him you're here. If he wants to meet with you, he'll come to the room. If not, I will come and tell you to leave."

"I'll take that hand." Sam nodded.

Grace escorted Sam to the empty room which contained only a desk and two chairs. She'd been considering offering it to Chase. Once she deposited Sam, Grace headed to Paul's office, planning how much she'd tell him while she walked down the hall. She leaned against his doorway when she arrived and said, "We all have baggage, Dad. Sam is Chase's. This is personal and we need to let him deal with it."

"Did I hear my name?" Chase came down the hall toward her.

"Yes, Chase you did." Grace turned toward him. "Someone named Sam Young is here, and he's claiming he's your dad."

CHAPTER TEN

What? Shit! How did the bastard find me? "Sam Young is here in this building?" Chase asked, trying to process what he'd heard.

"I put him in an empty office to wait," Grace answered. "If you don't want to see him, stay here, and I'll tell him to leave."

"No." Chase put up a hand. "I'll take care of it."

"The end of my hall." Grace took his hand. "I'll be in my office if you need me." She kissed him right in front of her dad.

Chase noticed Paul winced as he left the room, but he'd deal with him later. He thought of every swear word he could as he walked toward his destination, fighting down the growing rage inside him. He slammed a hand on either side of the doorway of the occupied room and stared at his dad sitting in a chair. An older, sadder version of himself. "What the hell do you want, and how did you find me?"

"Chase!" Sam looked happy to see him.

Of course, he's happy. The ATM has arrived. "I said, what do you want?"

Sam slumped back in the chair. "I need money, Chase. It's not what you think."

"Oh, okay, what should I think?"

His dad held up his hands which slightly shook. "For this. I don't know why they started to shake. It started a few months ago."

"You can't pick up cards, I take it?" Chase stared at him, knowing his father lived and breathed gambling. He'd want to find out what was wrong to get back to his life's work.

"You're right, but I thought nothing of it until Ginny…"

"Ginny?"

"My … friend said maybe I need to go to a doctor."

"You have no money saved or a real job with insurance." Chase wasn't asking, he knew the answer.

"No." Sam glanced up and tried to make eye contact. Chase looked away. "Son," he said.

"Don't call me that! You only do when you want money. How much this time?"

"Enough for the doctor and tests."

"Send me the bills."

"I don't know where you live, Chase."

"Someone will contact you, as always."

"Your sweet little secretary, Bobbie?"

Bobbie was his dad's age, but Chase wouldn't share the information. "Yeah, Bobbie will call you."

"All right, that's all I can ask." Sam stood and came toward Chase, arms extended, but Chase stepped away from the doorway to let him pass.

"Never come here again and stay out of my life," Chase hissed. "Do you understand? Bobbie will give you a number to call if you need anything else." He'd always had the contact number blocked. Sam wasn't given addresses or phone numbers, but somehow, he always managed to track Chase down at work. *At least he never found the house.* "I expect test results, too, Sam."

"You'll get them."

"Did you hear me? Promise to never show up here again."

"I won't, dammit, but I don't get it. Why here? Doing community service or something?" Sam chuckled.

"Yeah, Sam, that's what I'm doing. It's called none of your business." Chase's blood pumped through his veins at record speed. His heart pounded so hard, he didn't know if he could get it back to a normal beat. "Get out."

Chase watched his father's back until it disappeared around the corner. He followed until he was sure Sam left the building. When he turned, Grace stood close to him. Two strides, and he had her in his arms. "Thank you."

"You trusted me enough to share some secrets." Grace kissed his lips. "Now, I need a little more information."

Chase went with her theory once they settled into her office. "Yes, I changed my name, hoping Sam wouldn't find me." He wanted to distract her from the name, Chase Young. Grace may recognize it from aviation magazines or newspaper articles once she thought about it. How would he explain he had the same name as a billionaire?

"He's quite the detective." Grace lifted the corners of her mouth. "Sorry, he found you. Did you give him money?"

"Not exactly." Chase explained he would cover the medical bills. Once he spoke with Bobbie, he'd tell her to wire Sam some cash. *Why do I give in so easily?*

"I noticed his hands shook when I spoke with him," Grace said. "Something might be wrong. It's best to find out. You did the right thing."

"At the end of the day, he is my dad. I won't let him be destitute."

"I'm surprised you're not asking for a raise." Grace teased.

"Give it to Tim instead." Chase smiled and saw the perfect opportunity to change the subject. "Hey, won't Tim and Jen get our delivery today?"

"You mean the present from me?" Grace pressed her lips together. "I wish you'd let me put your name on the card."

"We'll tell them one day when we're old and gray." Chase winked. "Do I have an assignment, or should I go home and take you with me?"

"Don't go yet, although I love the offer. Paul is working on your schedule."

"I'll go talk to him." Chase pulled her into his arms, wanting one more kiss and a whiff of her perfume. "Dinner?"

"Yes," she breathed. "And sleep over. My place."

"What's wrong with mine?"

"Mine's nicer, and my stuff's there." Grace hugged him.

"I'll let you know my schedule as soon as I get it."

Chase avoided the Fed Ex guy at the doorway, maneuvering around him as he deposited a few boxes outside Grace's office. "Do you always give such good service?" Chase asked him, thinking how delivery people couldn't wait to drop off at the nearest stop and be on their way.

"I don't mind," the guy answered. "Grace gets all the packages and signs. Once I'm in the building, I head straight here."

"I'll leave you to it." Chase saluted and headed for Paul's office. Grace had grounded him after his encounter with Sam, and he was happy she took his side. *Sweet, sweet Grace.*

"Chase," Paul said, looking up as he entered. "Grace has convinced me to give you another chance."

"Thanks, Paul." *Otherwise my assignment is blown.*

"I want to put you back on the Miami flight."

"What? I thought it was Mark's."

"He wants easy, Chase, but I need him to go bigger and want to learn more. Mark needs varied experiences because one day he'll run the airline with his siblings. Tim's had a variety of tasks thrown at him over the years, even after the first two girls were born. He missed a lot of time with them. Now, we've tried to give him a better schedule. Did you hear I'm going to have a grandson?"

"I did."

"From Grace?"

Chase nodded. *Here it comes.*

"Don't hurt her."

A curdling scream came down the hall. "Grace!" Chase charged from the office, running to her. "What is it?" He felt Paul's presence behind him.

"This!" Grace pointed down into a huge box on her desk. "A dead falcon!"

Chase rounded her desk and pulled her away from the box.

"Gracie," Paul said. "I forgot to tell you. I ordered a stuffed falcon from a taxidermist for the lobby."

Chase looked at the bird, and its neck appeared broken. Speckles of blood covered its beak. "If that's true, you better call them. Whoever did this, did a shit job."

"Let me see…" Paul gasped and took a step back when he peered over the edge. "Good god, man, why would someone send a dead bird to our office?"

"To tell you Falcon won't be flying the skies in the coming days," Chase answered. He stared at Paul. "Now do you believe me?"

"What's the return address?"

Chase searched the box. "There is none." He turned to Grace, who stood motionless in the corner of her office. "Are you okay?"

"Please get it out of here."

Chase started for the box, but Paul beat him to it. "This needs to go in the trash." He shook his head. "I'll make doubly sure this isn't from the taxidermist. When I find out, I'll get back to you."

"I'd appreciate it." Chase took Grace in his arms. "Let me get you out of here, if only for an hour. Fresh air, bright sunshine might help the mood. We'll get breakfast and come back."

Grace nodded against his chest and he felt her body slightly trembling. "I'm okay. I was startled. It makes little sense. Why would anyone do this? No one could scare us into giving up the company."

"It's a bold gesture, Grace. Someone thinks you're already sunk or close to it." Chase could tell her many stories of corporate espionage, people hired to tank companies and other illicit business practices. "If someone is interested in the company, they should make a legitimate offer instead of using intimidation tactics or creating chaos."

"Nicely said." Grace gave him one of her wonderful smiles.

"You know what I will do to you tonight?" He teased.

"No, what?" Her lashes fluttered.

"Kiss you everywhere until you beg me to stop."

"And if I don't?" Grace slipped her arm through his.

"It could be a long night."

* * * *

Chase kept his promise and returned Grace to the front door of the office in an hour. They made plans to meet later, giving him time to investigate. If he had the means, he'd break into Paul's house and move on to Mark's apartment. Hell, he'd even visit Tim and Jen's house if he thought he'd get away with it. *I have the perfect excuse!*

In minutes, after pulling off the road, he had Tim's address in an upper-class neighborhood outside Charlotte. He drove until he arrived at what looked like a recently finished housing development. The sprawling Tudor and colonial style homes had stone or brick fronts with manicured yards. "This needs upkeep, Tim. Can you afford it? Why sabotage your job?" There was a missing piece to Tim's puzzle.

Chase hoped Tim was home. He wanted to see the look on his face when he told him of the dead falcon sent to the office. Watching the addresses as he drove, he found the house and pulled in the driveway. "Showtime."

A little girl with two missing front teeth answered the door. A screened one was still between them, which Chase assumed was locked. "Hi. Mommy said to wait. Daddy's almost ready."

Chase looked down and realized he wore his pilot's uniform. He'd dressed in case he was given a flight. "Oh, I'm not here to pick him up. I want to talk to him."

"Mommy says to wait."

Chase realized they had a security system and Jen was communicating with her daughter. "Sure." He heard footsteps, and Tim appeared before him.

"Thanks, Sara." Tim rubbed his daughter's head. "She gets a kick out of answering the door if we know who it is. Otherwise, the person can stand here forever, and we won't answer." He unlocked the screen door. "Come in." He wrinkled his brow. "Or should I ask why you're here?"

"Is it okay to talk?" Chase gestured to Sara.

"Sara, go upstairs with Mommy and the girls."

"Okay!" Sara skipped to the stairs.

Chase wanted to make sure she made it to the second floor before he spoke. "Something strange happened at Falcon today and I thought you should know."

Tim's eyebrows raised, but he said nothing.

"Grace opened a box and found a dead falcon inside. Its neck broken."

"What the hell!" Tim threw out his hands.

Chase studied every movement and gesture Tim made. He genuinely seemed surprised, even when caught off-guard with the surprise visit. "Paul and Grace don't know who sent it. Do you?"

"What?" Tim's face registered alarm as he took a step back. "Did you come over here to accuse me of something again?"

"No, Tim, I'm not accusing you of anything. You have to admit, sitting at your sister's desk after hours looked suspicious, but you told me why you were there."

"Confidentially." Tim crossed his arms. "And, to get you off my back, I am forced to tell you something else. I got an offer, a good one, from a major airline but, I didn't take it. If Jen knew, she'd have my head. I'm loyal to my dad and Falcon. That's why I asked Grace for a raise. We can afford it."

"No, *we* can't." Chase stared hard at Tim. He wanted to accept his explanation and decided he would. "Confidentially?"

Tim lifted one side of his mouth. "Yeah."

"I'm dating your sister."

"I get it. Go on."

"She's been working night and day on the books. Something doesn't add up if you're doing so well."

"What? There are financial problems? No one told me." Tim looked truly shocked. "I'd never ask for more money if I knew that."

"That's not it, Tim. Falcon *is* doing well. Someone's out to get the company, either for themselves or do in the competition."

"Hell, no!"

Satisfied, Chase turned to leave.

"Chase, if I can do anything, let me know, and thanks for coming out here to tell me."

In the car, Chase crossed Tim off his list, but not Paul. *Paul could have sent the bird.* "One down, who is left?"

Beside Paul, he'd have a chat with Ray tomorrow. He may let something slip. *Mark?* Chase waffled when it came to Grace's brother. A good detective looked for clues then proof. He had neither on Mark.

He'd made good time to Tim's which helped since he still had errands on his to-do list. His dad had to be dealt with and for that, he needed to go home and talk to Bobbie in person. The Honda had great gas mileage, so he didn't worry about filling up as he hopped on the interstate.

Chase laughed. "I'm beginning to like you." He slapped the car's dashboard. After parking in an outer spot by his garage, Chase got out and walked around to the back of his house, punching the button to connect to Mr. Smith.

"Hello, Mr. Young."

"Mr. Smith."

"What can I do for you this afternoon?"

"I would like my cellphone back. You're not taking theirs, so why mine?"

"You are doing well without it, no?"

"No, well yes, what the hell! Come on! I had a visit from my dad, and I could really use it."

"Do you believe him?"

"You know about his hands?" Chase wanted to throw his phone as far as he could.

"I do now. Are they shaking?"

"Doesn't that mean Parkinson's?"

"It could, but there are many reasons it could happen. Alcohol withdrawal for one."

"He's not an alcoholic."

"I see. Just a gambler."

"Shit! Dammit, yeah!" Chase forgot he was vetted. *This bastard knows everything.*

"Do you plan to help him?" Smith asked.

"I always do."

"As every good son should."

"What do you know except for what you read on paper or had your minions tell you?" Chase snarled. "I am not a good son. I loathe my father but will not let him starve."

"As I said …"

"Look, Smith, the reason I called is to get my cellphone. That's it."

"Let's wait a bit longer."

"Never mind. I gotta go. This conversation was pointless as usual."

"I wouldn't say that. Tim is off your list."

"Something tells me you know what's going on, Smith. Remember this. If we meet, my hands will be the first ones around your filthy neck. You probably sent the dead falcon just to taunt me." Chase snorted. "Wait! Is Grace in any kind of danger? Smith? Smith!" He threw the phone to the ground. Luckily, it landed in the grass.

"Chase!" Renata called. "What are you doing out here talking to yourself?"

He picked up the phone, walked toward the patio and found her straightening chairs. "Hey, let the help do that."

Renata straightened and placed her hands on her hips. "I am the help."

"No, you're the house manager. We agreed, remember?"

Renata plopped into a chair she'd moved back to position. "I need to do something, Chase. I get bored."

Chase sat opposite her. "No, you don't. Between scheduling, dealing with the staff, placing orders for groceries and household items, taking care of the dogs and cooking dinner, you have more than enough to fill the day as you requested." He leaned back against the seat cushion. "What's wrong?"

Renata let out a breath. "My daughter. She broke up with the *hijo de una hyena* for the second time as you are aware."

Chase threw his head back and laughed. "Did you call him a son of a hyena?" He slapped his leg.

"I did. I don't want to be caught in the middle of their relationship again. I like him. She wants me to come to Miami and spend time with her. We both know that is not the real reason."

"Your daughter wants your help to get him back?"

"No, she is done. Finished." Renata gave a nod of the head. She wants me to move back to Miami, have the family in one place again."

"Your older daughter still lives there, if I'm not mistaken."

"You mean the good one, Rosa? She married a wonderful man, has two lovely children." Renata crossed herself. "Who are in good health, smart and beautiful. What does the other one want?" She blew a puff of air. "A career."

"Nothing wrong with that, Renata." Chase chuckled. "You wanted the same thing."

"I left Miami because my husband died, Chase. I couldn't live there anymore. You seem to be the only one who understands."

"You know you are welcome here as long as you want, working for me or not."

"How could I leave my little bungalow you built for me on the grounds? The views are fantastic from every window." She winked.

Chase stood. "How about this? I won't be here this week. Invite both daughters, including Rosa's family and enjoy the place. They can use the basement suite."

"There's plenty of room for them."

"Not really. Use the basement."

"It's hard to call that beautiful apartment a basement." Renata scoffed. "Thank you for your kind offer."

"Call Craig. Make arrangements through him personally. Tell him I said to get those daughters here ASAP." Chase walked to the sunroom entrance. "Renata, is Bobbie here?"

"Yep, every Monday through Friday, Chase. She comes in at eight on the dot."

"Good, I need to speak with her." Chase walked through his kitchen, designed with an open floor plan and built for entertainment. When he reached the great room, he called, "Bobbie?"

"I'm coming, Chase." She appeared at the entrance to the hall. "What's up?"

"My dad … Sam. Appears he has something wrong with him and needs money for a doctor."

"Like hell he does!"

CHAPTER ELEVEN

"Bobbie, come, sit." Chase swept his hand toward the light gray leather sectional. "Put your feet up."

"If you want me to put my feet up, it's bad." Bobbie huffed. "Do I need to call your mama? Is it that bad?"

"No!" Chase held up his hands. "Whatever you do, don't tell my mom."

Bobbie and his mom had become friends during the Red years when they both worked as inside sales reps at the same company. Chase had known her since he was ten years old. She'd always dyed her hair red, and he was unsure of the real color. Bobbie always wore makeup and used her savings for Botox injections, salon treatments and expensive haircuts. The total opposite of his mom, but he trusted her with his personal business.

After he explained Sam's visit, Bobbie covered her mouth in shock. "You don't think…?"

"He's ill? Has a chronic disorder?" Chase shook his head. "I don't know."

"I'll deal with it all. Did he give you a phone number?"

"No," Chase answered. "I assume he has the same one." He bit into his bottom lip. "Do me a favor. Find out how he knew where I was. He never said."

Bobbie flipped her long, red curls over her shoulder. "I don't even know where you go, Chase. Mind sharing?"

"Not yet, but soon."

"It has something to do with an airline," Bobbie said, waving her hand from the top of his head to his feet.

Shit! I forgot I was wearing the uniform. "Yeah, I'm doing a good deed." *Might as well use the excuse Sam gave me.*

"That is so sweet, Sugar! I want to pinch your cheeks right now."

"Please don't." Chase chuckled.

Bobbie leaned forward, squinting. She took the glasses that dangled from a chain around her neck and slipped them on. "Falcon?"

"A buddy asked me to fill in for him as a favor. He had a last-minute emergency. Think of me as the substitute teacher." Chase stood and helped Bobbie from the sofa. "See what you can discover. Have him send the bills to the P.O. box we established and wire him three thousand."

"Dollars?" Bobbie widened her eyes. "Okay, and I'll look into how he found you. When was the last time you saw him? Six months ago?"

"You're the one who keeps track." Chase kissed her cheek. "Remember, don't tell Mom until we know something more."

"You know I won't. The relationship you got with your daddy is not Maureen's concern anymore. You're a grown man, Chase. A good, solid, decent one. Don't forget that."

"Thanks, and I don't take that lightly. You saw me in my teen years." Chase hugged her. "Watch the store while I'm gone."

"Always do, Sugar."

Chase wiped at the corner of his eye as he walked to the garage. He had two great women in his life watching out for him and not taking advantage of him. But here was Sam, showing up at Falcon with his hand out. Funny, if his dad really knew him, he'd know he'd never need to beg for money. His family and friends never did. He took care of their needs, expenses and more.

The Honda felt like a steam bath when Chase hopped in. "I should have parked in the garage. I didn't know I would be this long. Let's crank up the air." He looked down at his clothes, decided to go to his apartment and call Grace from there. He checked the time. *Three p.m. I've got time.*

The apartment started to feel like a comfortable place. He spent little time there, but it was a good base. Chase hopped in the shower, found clean clothes and hung the uniform on a hangar to take with him. He sent a text to Grace and said he'd bring dinner to her condo, teasing her by saying they could eat by the pool. *The pool.* Her smooth, soft skin and the way she tasted flooded his mind.

A pound at the door startled him back to reality. "Perfect! Are you in there?"

"Hang on a minute, Darcy!" he yelled from the bathroom and slipped on a white shirt, rolling up the sleeves. Chase hesitated in front of the mirror. *Didn't Sam wear a white shirt? No time to change.*

"Perfect!" Two more bangs.

"I'm coming." Chase skidded to a stop in front of his door and opened it. "What is so urgent?"

"What did you do? Do you know someone at this college or on their board?" Darcy waved a letter in his face.

"What you're talking about?" Chase ran his hand through his hair. "Start from the beginning."

"I got this letter from UNC." Darcy slapped his chest with the paper. "No one knows I want to go to college, and my mom started a fund…except you." She glared at him. "I am not your charity case!"

"May I?" Chase held out his hand and studied the return address. "University of North Carolina-Charlotte. Impressive." *Smith works fast. I give him credit.* "Do you mind if I read the letter?"

"Sure, do whatever you want." Darcy folded her arms over her chest.

"Duh, duh, duh," he said as he read through the information. "Duh, duh, duh."

"Will you stop saying that?" Darcy hissed. "Get to the under-served part of the community. They're talking about me."

The letter stated Darcy qualified for a scholarship given to worthy candidates who hadn't continued their education past high school. It said names were obtained from schools in the area and cross-checked for college enrollment. It didn't outright give Darcy the scholarship. She'd have to work for it.

Chase cleared his throat. "From what I read, you've been chosen from a list of high school grads who *may* qualify for a scholarship. I had nothing to do with it. It appears someone recently funded the program." He stared at her. "Does it look like I have that kind of money?"

Darcy studied him for a long minute. "Okay, sorry. Last week I told you my story, and this week I get the letter." Darcy dropped her eyes. "Do you think I'm good enough?"

"Darcy, if you don't fill out the application, I'll do it for you." Chase placed a finger under her chin and lifted until their eyes met. "I'm proud of you."

"It's in town. I can keep the apartment and maybe one job."

"Sounds like a plan. What will you major in?"

"Business. I always thought I had good business sense."

"When you graduate, I know someone who will give you a job."

"Really?" Darcy's face relaxed, and she returned to the woman he'd grown to know.

"Yeah, really."

* * * *

Chase whistled as he walked up the pathway to Grace's condo. A bottle of wine in one hand, takeout in the other, he hoped she was watching for him or he'd have to knock with an elbow or knee, but he door opened at the right moment.

Grace stood in the doorway, radiating happiness. She'd gotten some sun and Chase longed to discover her tan lines. She wore no makeup and the fresh face look suited her. "Let me help." She took the wine bottle. "Is patio dining okay?"

"Anywhere is fine." Chase kissed her cheek as he came inside. "I saw Darcy today."

"Really?" Grace pulled out a drawer and found the opener.

"She got a letter in the mail. Someone's funding a program for people in need who want to go to college and didn't get the chance."

Grace frowned. "I never heard of a program like that. How did they find her?"

"It said through school recommendations. She still has to apply and get accepted."

"I'm happy for her. I can find something for her at Falcon. She won't need to work nights at the Golden Swan." Grace popped the cork. "I assumed she still needs to work."

"That's sweet of you." Chase grabbed two wine flutes, the bottle and headed toward her sliding doors.

The patio had a shade awning and surrounded by greenery making it cool and private. A table for four sat left to the middle with a loveseat and chair in the opposite corner. Chase turned to go back inside, nearly bumping into Grace. "You're fast." He took the tray and set it on the table.

"I dreamed of having a romantic dinner out here one day, but never did." Grace sighed.

"Now you are." Chase kissed her neck as he helped her to her seat.

"Did you know you're back on the Miami route?" Grace asked.

"Paul and I were discussing it when you…"

"Screamed?" Grace smiled. "Why, Chase? I can't stop thinking about it. Being in the red since January was bad enough, but the bad press with hashtag scare in the air and a dead falcon is giving me an eerie feeling. It's like someone's trying to scare us besides financially attack us." She pursed her lips. "Sorry, I shouldn't be talking shop during our lovely dinner."

No, you should. That's why I'm here. "I don't mind going over details with you. Any progress with the books?"

"I am finding some discrepancies, although at first I wrote them off as price increases." Grace shook her head. "Enough shop talk. I'll work on it tomorrow. I'd like to enjoy this gorgeous evening and the man who's spending it with me."

When they finished dinner, Grace led Chase to the loveseat. She curled up next to him and they sat snuggled against each other until the sun set.

"Tired?" Chase asked.

"No, I feel relaxed." Grace chuckled. "And with all that's going on at work, I shouldn't be."

"What if I carry you to bed, and we don't sleep?"

"You promised to kiss every part of my body." Grace looked up at him with her beautiful chestnut eyes and Chase swept her into his lap.

The kiss he gave her was meant to last until he got her into the bedroom but somehow Grace had removed his shirt and was now working on his pants.

"Do you want me to trip and fall as I carry you to your room?" Chase teased, whispering in her ear. "Besides, I need time to remove your dress."

"It's all I'm wearing," she whispered into his ear, and with that, Chase whisked her to the bedroom.

* * * *

Chase woke the same time as Grace did. The flight to Miami was at eight and he wanted to talk to Ray, the head technician, before he left. She had said she wanted to leave at seven and he wanted a jump on her.

Grace had joined him in the shower, and he promised coffee and bagels while she dried her hair. Chase kept an eye on the clock, wanting to be out the door at six.

"You're in such a hurry today, Chase. You'll beat me out the door." Grace wrapped her arms around his waist and rested her head on his back. "You smell good."

"You smell better." Chase turned and kissed her. "I guess I'm a little nervous after what happened last time. I want to be at the gate early, check out the plane, talk to the mechanics …"

"Okay, I get it." Grace placed a finger over his mouth. "Want me to come along?"

"No, I'll be fine." Chase pushed the toaster lever down, picked the bagel setting and poured coffee.

"I was thinking about Darcy," Grace said.

"Platonically, I hope."

"Stop." Grace giggled. "I hope she gets the scholarship."

"She will."

"You seem sure." Grace tilted her head. "I feel you are keeping something from me."

"Me?" Chase widened his eyes. "Never." He slipped onto a kitchen barstool next to her and nudged her. "We'll tag team her, make sure she fills out the application."

"Okay." Grace nodded. "Meet at your place tonight? If she's not home, we'll go to the Golden Swan."

"I like the way you think." Chase wiped his mouth and kissed Grace on the way by. "I'll see you tonight."

"Don't forget to brush your teeth!" Grace teased.

"Never do!" He called over his shoulder, raced to the bathroom and out the door when he'd finished.

Grace lived a short distance from the airport and Chase reached his destination in twenty minutes. Parking the Honda in the spots reserved for Falcon against the side of the hangar, he hopped from the car and strode to the huge opening. Voices came from the building, men and women already at work, preparing planes for their daily flights. Chase headed for the head technician's office, hoping Ray was there.

Chase let out a silent thanks when he saw Ray behind the desk. He knocked and waited even though the door was wide open.

"Come in, door's always open. You guys know that …" Ray wore a look of surprise when he looked up from his paperwork. "I didn't expect a visit from the pilot today. Chase, right?" He stood and extended his hand. "Did you come to punch my lights out?" He laughed, but to Chase, it sounded as if he was nervous.

"No, but I would like to discuss the plane I'll be flying today and talk about the one you put back into service."

"Not a problem." Ray waved his hand at the door. "Let's walk."

Chase followed Ray out the door into the hangar.

"We'll take the plane over to the gate at eight-fifteen," Ray said. "I've checked it at least five times. I'll swear on my mother's family bible I signed off on the plane you flew as fit to fly, and the one you'll use today is safe for travel."

Swear on his mother's family bible? Must be a thing. Chase waffled, trying to decide if Ray told the truth. "Who has access to the hangar beside the people who work here?"

"I can't vouch for everyone who comes and goes, it's a busy place. I don't work here twenty-four seven, although it feels like I do." Ray chuckled. "People who visit are supposed to check in so I know who's been here. And if I don't know, my assistant does."

Would someone who's guilty offer that much information? "Who is your assistant?"

"Candance." Ray cocked his head toward a smaller office next to his. "Everyone says she has a crush on me." He shrugged. "Not my type."

No, Grace is your type. Chase glanced toward the office, the top half made of plexiglass, and a chubby young woman wiggled her fingers at him. She had bleach blonde hair, dressed well and her makeup wasn't over the top. "She seems friendly." Chase didn't know what else to say. "And you said, she'd report anyone unusual coming around, especially at closing time or after hours."

"If she was here, yes."

"Is someone always in the building?"

Ray dipped his head. "Always. We got a skeleton crew late at night who keep to themselves, and if there's a big problem, they call me. Jackie's in charge. She's been with Paul since the early years." He lifted a shoulder. "She prefers to work nights."

Chase made a mental note to find out about Jackie and talk to Candance when he found time. "What do you think happened to those seats?"

"Someone loosened them. I tightened them myself. Sat and bounced in them. From my lips to God's ear." Ray pointed to the sky.

"Do you think Paul came onto the plane after inspection and loosened them?"

"What?" Ray covered his heart with the palm of his hand. "That's blasphemy. This here is Paul's life. He put blood, sweat and tears into the company. If I had the ability, I'd fire you right on the spot." He crossed his arms.

"I'm sorry, Ray. I had to ask. I'm trying to help Grace and Paul sort this out."

"Why didn't you say that in the first place?" Ray placed his hand on Chase's shoulder. "Between you and me, someone wants this company. Too many odd things happened over the past months. We've had tools disappear, even the work schedule. I had to call guys in on short notice because someone didn't show up for work. When I finally get a chance to give the worker hell, they tell me they weren't on the schedule."

"Did you tell Paul?"

"Some of it. He's got enough to worry about."

"Like ordering refurbished parts and cutting other expenses?" Chase asked.

"You know about that?"

"Paul told me." Chase still wanted to keep Paul on his list of suspects, but Ray appeared to be a loyal employee, doing as he was told. *Ray, my boy, you're off the list.* "Do me a favor, Ray. If anything unusual happens, will you call me or Grace? Don't bother Paul. He's overwhelmed right now."

"I will. I can even go to headquarters and talk with Grace."

"That won't be necessary."

Ray stared at him, a wounded look in his eyes.

"If it's important, I guess you will," Chase replied, and Ray's shoulders relaxed. "I've got to get over to the airport. Thanks for all your help."

"Plane should be right as rain, Chase. I'm like Santa, checking his list twice."

Chase smiled, hoping to end the conversation. "I'm sure everything will be fine."

CHAPTER TWELVE

Grace paced in her office, worrying for no reason. "I could go to the hangar, not the airport, and talk with Ray. Double check on the plane." She let her secretary know she'd be there and would return later that morning.

"If something happened to Chase because of Falcon problems, I'd never forgive myself," she said as she slid behind the wheel of her car. She'd waited until eight, after rush hour, to drive to the airport. "Chase has to be in the air by now and will never know I'm checking up on him."

None of cars parked by the hangar looked familiar. Glad her brothers and dad were somewhere else, Charlotte walked to the building. They'd question why she was there, and she didn't have an excuse ready. Grace hurried toward the entrance, heading straight to Ray's office. She saw he wasn't there, but someone occupied the small office next to it. "Candance?" She stopped in the doorway.

The woman looked up from her computer. "Hello, Grace. What brings you down here?"

"Ray."

Candance looked as if Grace had punched her. *Or maybe she wants to punch me?* "Are you all right, Candance?"

"Yes, fine. Something I ate." Candance picked up a pen. "Do you want to leave a message?"

"Sure, if he's not here."

"Grace!"

"Ray?" Grace turned to face him.

"You looked surprised to see me."

"I was telling her you had stepped out," Candance answered.

"I never step out." Ray shook his head and smiled at Grace. "What can I do for you?"

"I wanted to check on the plane you sent over for the Miami flight. It's not the one we used for the inaugural flight, is it?"

"No, I got that baby in the hangar going over it with a fine-tooth comb."

Grace smiled as she thought of the sayings Ray liked to use. Her brothers found it annoying, but she thought it was endearing. Sometimes, she thought Ray made things up, as if they were passed down from generation to generation. She especially like his mother's family bible story. Ray liked to bring it up whenever he wanted someone to know he told the truth. "Thanks for that, Ray. I'd like to know more about it."

"Come into my office where we can talk," Ray said, bowing at the waist, arm extended, motioning for Grace to go first.

"Thanks for your help, Candance." Grace tried to make eye contact with her, but she appeared busy.

"Anytime," Candance said under her breath.

"Can I get you coffee? A doughnut?" Ray gestured at the seat in front of his desk.

"I'm fine."

"You're the second visitor I've had today."

I thought he might stop by. "Chase? Checking on his plane?"

"Yes, I assured him he was in good hands." Ray placed his hands together, cupping them. "Like the commercial." He stared at her. "You know the one?"

"Sure," Grace answered, recalling why she could never go out with Ray again. One long night had been enough. She hoped he wasn't going to ask her now. *You have a boyfriend, girl! Let him ask.* Grace was dying to tell someone, but Ray wasn't a good choice.

"Paul keeps telling me to get it back in service, Grace," Ray said. "But I want a walk-through with him or one of your brothers. I need witnesses."

"No one's blaming you, Ray."

"Chase doesn't trust me, Grace. Why did you hire him in the first place?"

"I didn't. Paul did."

"Oh." Ray tapped the tips of his fingers together. "Are … you … seeing him?"

"We're dating if that's what you mean." Grace bit into her lower lip.

"All righty then." Ray hopped up from his chair. "I've got to get back to work and I'm sure you do, too."

Grace draped her arm over his shoulder when she stood. "You're doing a great job, Ray." As they walked out of his office, she dropped her arm and out of nowhere, Ray pulled her into a hug.

"Thanks for believing in me."

"Any time." Flustered, Grace pulled away and out of the corner of her eye, she saw Candance staring at them through her office window, her eyes shooting daggers at Grace.

After taking a few steps, Grace stopped. *Is Ray blind? Do I play matchmaker?* Her life felt so full she wanted to help someone having the same feeling. "Ray?" She turned.

"Yes?" Ray closed the gap between them. "You should ask out Candance."

"You're the second person who's brought her up today." Ray blew out a breath.

"I think she likes you," Grace whispered.

"As I've said, not my type." Ray shook his head. "Have a good day, Grace. Stop by anytime."

"I'm a big help," Grace mumbled as she unlocked the car and got in. She checked the time. *Nine. Chase should almost be in Miami.*

Something inside her longed to be on that plane, make sure nothing happened. Grace couldn't stop thinking of Chase until she got to the office. "I need a distraction and the accounting books will do it."

* * * *

"Chase?" Halle gave him a shove. "Do you want to get coffee?"

"What? Yeah, sure." He'd done it again. Daydreamed. This time he deserved the chance to slip away. He wanted to think about Grace and couldn't wait to call her.

Halle winked at him. "Follow me. I know a place. There's food, too. And you can call her from there."

"I didn't talk about Grace the whole flight, did I?" Chase exclaimed in mock disbelief.

"No, but I get to talk about Kyle on the flight back."

It felt good to be back in the air with Halle. They had a smooth flight and planned to turn around and do it again in an hour. Back in Charlotte, he'd have less than a two-hour window before doing it one more time. Paul had bumped the afternoon flight up an hour after going over first week details. It gave him less time, but the hangar was close.

"I'll buy," Halle said. "You get a table."

Chase picked one away from the crowd, signaled Halle and pulled out his phone. "Grace?"

"I'm here."

"I'm in Miami."

"No kidding." She laughed.

"I've got a little time when I get back. I'd love to meet up with you, but I know you're busy. Keep working on the puzzle, and so will I. I have an idea."

"What?" Grace sounded excited.

"Let's wait until I have what I'm looking for. We're still meeting at my place tonight. Damn, I need to give you a key."

"Call when you leave the airport. I'll meet up with you."

"And, baby?"

"Yes, Chase?" she breathed into the phone.

"I'll think of you while I'm away." Chase hated to end the call. "I should be at the apartment by seven-thirty."

"I'll wait for your call."

"Tell her I said hi." Halle set a bag and two coffees on the table.

"She already hung up," Chase said. "I'll tell her when I see her later tonight."

"Uh-huh." Halle stared at him. "Remember, I'm watching you. She's my girl and if you hurt her…"

"I promise I won't." Chase rubbed the side of his jaw. He had secrets and didn't know if any of them would hurt Grace. When the time came, would she think he was a liar or using her? He had to convince her otherwise now, prove he was sincere. "Can I confide in you?"

"Yes, Chase, and I'm not even going to tease you. Yes, you can."

"I picture Grace as someone I want in my life forever. I hope we are headed down that path, but it's too early to tell."

"Makes sense." Halle pretended to zip her mouth. "She won't hear it from me. But, it's a good line. Use it tonight." She winked.

"God, Halle! Can you ever be serious?" Chase laughed.

"You saw it, for one rare moment."

Chase enjoyed his break with Halle, the time went quickly, and they were back in Charlotte by noon. After the passengers deplaned, he took the stairs down to the tarmac to talk to the groundcrew. "Is anyone going to the hangar?"

"I am." One woman raised her hand. She jumped in a golf cart and waved for him to join her.

"I guess it's lunch hour, right?" Chase asked.

"For some." She nodded.

Chase needed to talk to Candance alone in her office yet didn't know lunch protocol. *Shifts, take turns, all go at once?* He'd soon find out.

"Thanks." Chase hopped from the cart as it came to a stop.

"I'm going back in about fifteen minutes," the woman said. "If you want a ride back."

"I do," Chase answered. "Don't leave without me." He glanced at Ray's office. *Empty.* Candance's was next. *Please be there.*

Candance sat at her desk eating a sandwich, the paper that had been wrapped around it spread out as a placemat. Chase winced as sauce dripped from the bun onto the desk. *Maybe I should wait. Let her finish.* He spotted a soda machine and headed for it, needing to pass by her office. "Hello, Candance." He waved. "Would you like a soda?"

"Any type of cola is fine." Candance waved.

Chase took his time at the machine, bought a water and a cola. He cracked open his bottle, took a few swigs and returned the cap. Candance was balling up the paper when he arrived at her door.

"What brings you here?" Candance smiled.

"I wanted to tell Ray in person we had a smooth flight."

"He's usually here but forgot his lunch."

"He packs?"

"Yep." Candance nodded. "Doesn't like to spend his money. He's a saver, to quote him."

"What about you? Spender or saver?"

"Spender, of course." She waved her hand over the front of her body. "Can't you tell?"

"I can." Chase chuckled. "Do you mind if I ask you something?"

"Sure."

"Are you one of those eight-to-five workers or don't mind putting in overtime."

"Since you saw me earlier this morning, I am a seven-to-four girl, but it never works out that way. I usually stay an extra hour. Sometimes Ray tells me to come in later if I'm needed till six."

"Ray says a smaller crew comes in for the night shift."

"Shifts." Candance held up two fingers. "People come in at three and four p.m. staying till eleven. Then the skeleton crew comes in to relieve them and works till Ray gets here around six a.m. They're usually gone by the time I come in."

"You observe a lot and know what's going on, Candance. Besides having good business skills, those are excellent qualities."

"They are?"

"Absolutely." Chase hoped he had her warmed up for the big question. "Anyone ever come in that you don't recognize?"

"Sure, all the time, but they have to sign in…unless they're with Mr. Edison."

"Oh. Good to know." Chase pretended to turn to leave and then change his mind. "Has Mr. Edison ever shown up with someone after the main crew and Ray have left for the day?"

"I'm rarely here by myself." Candance shook her head. "Although a few months ago, Ray had an emergency. They took his grandma to the hospital. He asked me to stay, lock up our offices and make sure the night crew had what they needed."

Chase longed to check his watch, needing to get back to the airport. *Am I on to something or not?*

Candance tapped her chin. "Funny you should ask, but Mr. Edison showed up that day with someone he didn't introduce." She lifted a shoulder. "It's not my business. I only work here."

"What did the person look like? I may know him. It might be the pilot they interviewed before I got hired."

"Some guy who looked to be in his forties. Blonde hair, no make that dirty blonde hair, you know the look?" She didn't wait for Chase to respond. "A mustache, average height and build. He wore a wedding ring."

She described a hundred guys in the city. Chase shook his head. "Don't know him. I guess I should be going."

"There was one more thing. Mr. Edison asked that I not mention his visit to Ray. Not a big deal, he said, showing my friend around. When I protested, he said he'd do me a favor. He'd put in a good word for me with Ray. I don't know how that man knew I like Ray, but it was worth a shot. He also said since I've put in extra hours, he'd do something about that. On my birthday, I got a card from Falcon with five hundred dollars in it! Cash!"

"That all sounds very nice."

Candance hung her head. "Only he didn't put in a good word for me. Ray never asked me out."

Chase looked at his watch, not wanting to touch the subject. "Oh, look at the time. I do need to get back. Nice chatting with you, Candance."

"Thanks for the cola." Candance held the bottle in the air.

"Pilot! I'm leaving!"

"Coming!" Chase jogged to the cart where the flight mechanic already sat behind the wheel. On the ride back to the gate, he played the conversation over in his head. *Paul, you are guilty as hell. Bringing someone in after hours to help you sabotage the company. Now how do I tell Grace?*

* * * *

"What? No way!" Grace folded her arms across her chest. "You are blaming my dad for all of Falcon's problems?" she huffed and sat at Chase's dining table. "Find out who this mysterious dirty blonde-haired guy is." She shook her head. "I think Candance meant dark blonde but dirty makes him all the more sketchy. He may be the answer."

"Okay, fine. Where do we start?" Chase flipped back the cover to the pizza box. "Sorry, I'm hungry."

Grace reached for a piece and bit into it with force.

"That's it, take your aggression out on the pizza." Chase looked at her and smiled. "I don't want to accuse your dad of anything. I'm only relaying the story I heard from Candance. What about someone named Jackie on the night shift?"

"She goes way back with my dad, his first mechanic. No way would she turn on him."

"Okay, she's off the list. Let's get back to Candance's story of your dad and the blonde guy then. Think, Grace. Ray's called away, your dad assumes Candance left for the day, and the night crew doesn't pay attention. Perfect time to visit. But!" Chase held up his pointer finger. "One problem with the plan. Candance is still there, so, he bribes her to keep quiet."

"I can't picture my dad playing the part." Grace rested her elbow on the table, placing her head in her hand. "Wait a minute … Candance said Mr. Edison, not Paul."

"She did."

"Candance calls my dad and brothers, Mr. Edison." Grace smirked. "But, she always calls me Grace."

"That widens the search. We'd have to look for a man of that description with Paul, Tim or Mark. Although, I've taken Tim off the list."

"You did?" Grace breathed a sigh of relief. She wanted none of her family involved in this mess. She refused to accept the fact they could bring down the airline. "At what cost?"

"What do you mean?"

Grace blinked. "Did I say that aloud?"

"You said, 'at what cost'."

"If my dad or Mark wanted to hurt Falcon financially or cause its ruin, why? What would they get from it?"

"I agree. It makes no sense." Chase finished his pizza and wiped his hands. "I'll text Darcy and find out where she is tonight."

"I hope the bar," Grace replied. "I need a drink."

* * * *

"Perfect and Beauty. Did you come to tag team me?" Darcy wiped the bar with a cloth.

"Yes, we did," Grace answered. "Let me read the application."

"Do you think I carry it everywhere I go?" The piercing in Darcy's eyebrow appeared to vibrate. "I'll be right back." She disappeared and returned with the envelope. "Here. It's too many pages."

Chase tried to hide his shock. "May I see it?" He pulled the folded application from the envelope and examined the five-page document. *What was Smith thinking?*

"And, I need to write an essay." Darcy placed two beers in front of them.

"We can help, right, Chase?" Grace nudged him.

"Huh? Yeah, we can." He studied the questions and read the essay topic. "Write from your heart, Darcy. Tell why you want the scholarship, what you'll major in and how it will help you in life."

"That's all?"

"Don't listen to him, Darcy." Grace put her hand on Darcy's arm. "Except for the write your heart part. I have faith in you. You'll be coming to work for me."

"What?" Darcy pulled her arm from Grace's hand. "As a charity case?"

"Absolutely not. I heard you want to major in business. What better place to work and find out if it's your true calling? Besides, I'll work around your schedule if you get the scholarship."

Chase noticed Darcy had begun to tear up. She turned her back on them, acting busy at the cash register. "I've got to get a customer his bill. I'll be back."

"You got to her," Chase said, and slipped his arm around Grace's waist. He kissed her bare shoulder. "I … love … how you handled the situation." *Damn!* He wanted to say he loved her but not in the Golden Swan and so early in the relationship. Yet he did love her. Chase felt overwhelmed by the fact.

"And I … love … how you let me handle it." Grace's eyelashes fluttered.

She got it. She knows what I meant.

"Here's the deal," Darcy said when she returned. "I keep this job, give up the diner. Maybe work at Falcon."

"I say give it a try," Chase said. "We're on your side, Darcy."

"Why do you give a crap, Perfect?" Darcy glanced down the long bar. "No one in this bar does."

Chase looked at Grace. "I know a wise man who would probably say I am turning over a new leaf. I've been given a new lease on life."

Grace giggled. "Stop it. I feel like I'm out with Ray."

"Ray?" Darcy wiggled her eyebrows.

"Our head technician. If you come to work for me, you'll eventually meet him."

"Well, that was the missing piece!" Darcy laughed. "How can I refuse the offer?"

CHAPTER THIRTEEN

Chase had the day off. He'd worked Wednesday to Friday with an off day on Saturday. The schedule showed he worked again Sunday. He hoped to have the puzzle solved by then, say goodbye to Falcon and figure out how to keep Grace in his life.

He had two missions to complete. The first was to check in with Bobbie to get an update on his dad. The best place to call her was from his private airline company, C.Y. Airlines.

Beau had designed the logo, a pyramid with the C and Y inside. His Society buddy would let none of them hire out a job. If they did, Beau would examine the product, say it looked like crap and do it over. *No arguing with that man.* Chase chuckled. Beau also came up with a great tag line for Chase's company. 'See why you want to fly with us?' written in script across a picture of the inside a luxury jet. "Get it," he asked. "C.Y.?"

"Yeah, Beau, I got it." Chase never thought he'd own a jet, let alone a fleet, in three privately owned airfields across the country. He began the service when people asked him to fly them places on short notice. For the Society, he'd take them anywhere, anytime, but couldn't fulfill other requests. "That's when C.Y. was born," he said as he hopped from the car, taking in the buildings, hangars and runways.

"Mr. Young, I didn't expect you to come in today. Someone said you're off the grid."

Chase turned to greet one of his employees. "I'm never off the grid, Andy," he answered, patting the young man on the back as they walked from the parking lot.

Andy gestured to the Honda. "You are a little."

"The Honda? I can't give it up. One of the first cars I bought with my hard-earned cash," Chase answered, hoping Andy wouldn't question the model's year so he asked, "Summer classes start yet?"

"We had twenty sign up and start Monday."

The guy had been flying with his dad since he was three and got his license when he reached the age of sixteen. Andy knew planes inside and out, and Chase put him in charge of the flight school.

They parted at the entrance to the building, and Chase stopped to look around the office. No one sat behind the front desk, which was unusual, but most people were rarely in their workspace. He shrugged it off as he headed straight for his office. The opportunity gave him time to make a private call.

"Bobbie?"

"Oh, Chase, I am so glad you called. I've talked to your daddy, and he's got an appointment this afternoon. We might have test results by the end of the week."

"Did you ask him?"

"Calm down, Sugar, of course, I did. He said he got an anonymous tip. Even Sam thought it strange. But, he was ever grateful, Chase, cause of the shaking hands."

Damn Smith!

"Chase, Sugar, are you there?"

"Yes. Did you wire him the money?"

"Yes, I even found out where he lives."

That caught his attention. "Where?"

"In town."

"Not Vegas, Atlantic City?"

"You know you can gamble in about any state."

"I know, but those were his favorites. Do you know how long he's been here?"

"A year?"

"He moves closer to home when he thinks he's dying and needs help." Chase rubbed his temples.

"No one said he's dying," Bobbie answered. "I don't know if you thought of this, but I asked him to allow the doctor to speak with you and have access to all his tests. Otherwise, no deal."

"There's a reason I love you."

"You can't think of everything, Sugar, but you got your second mama watching out for you."

"Thanks, Bobbie."

"One more thing. How do I get a hold of you? Your cell goes straight to voicemail."

"I forgot to tell you, I lost track of my phone. I will buy a new one in a day or two."

"That's not good, Chase. Someone must have it because it's charged and taking messages."

Smith, you bastard. You've heard every single one, I'm sure.

"Don't worry, Bobbie. I'll call the phone store to cancel the old." Chase heard a noise in the hall. "Send me the name of Sam's doctor and any other info you feel I need to the C.Y. email account."

"You'll have it in five."

"Thanks, I'll talk to you soon." Chase looked up to see Craig in the doorway. "I haven't seen you in months." He rose from his chair, and they shook hands.

"We communicate more through texts and phone than in person I guess."

"There's something different about you." Chase shook his pointer finger. "Let me guess." *Shit, no!* He studied Craig carefully as Candance's description came back to him. *Forties, dark blonde hair, mustache, average height and build.* He glanced at Craig's left hand to double check. *Wedding ring.* "Mustache?"

"Yep, the wife hates it, but I like it."

"Take a seat." Chase motioned to a chair in the corner and sat on the loveseat crossways to it. "How are things going? I need to check in more often. Happy here?"

"Wow." Craig rubbed his face. "I can't believe you asked me that. I run this place." He spread out his arms. "As they say, what's not to like?"

"But, you don't own it."

Craig frowned. "It's the next best thing. Where's this coming from, Chase?"

"Nowhere. I thought I'd check with you and make sure everything's okay." Chase shrugged. *Can't show my hand yet. Damn, did I make a Sam reference?* He stood, the signal Craig was dismissed. "I'm waiting on an email. Once it comes through, I'll leave. Anything you want to go over?"

Craig hopped up from the chair, straightened his C.Y. Airlines polo and said, "I flew in Renata's daughters per your instructions."

"Great news. I'm sorry I told her to go straight to the top, but something's going on and she needed to see her daughters."

"So, you have a houseful?" Craig grinned.

"I'm not there this week. That's why I suggested it."

"Smart man." Craig patted Chase on the shoulder and left.

Chase returned to his desk, sat and opened his email, jotting down the information he needed. Pay phones were few and now he wished they were back on street corners and inside buildings like the old days. He could easily walk up to one and make a call. *Call! Oh, yes, Smith, I'm calling you.*

Still empty, the building gave him an eerie feeling as Chase left his office. *Where's the receptionist?* He looked over his shoulder, made a split-second decision to take advantage of the moment, and headed for Craig's office. His heart pounded as he pulled his phone from his pocket. *Does this damn thing take pictures? Yes!*

Craig's desk was an organized mess. He'd stacked piles of papers and folders all over the top. Chase didn't want to move a thing, looking over receipts, notes and documents as best he could. His eyes came to rest on a lone piece of paper tucked under the phone. He tugged it out, swallowed hard and took a picture. A glance at the door, he slid the note back where he found it and slipped from the room.

"Hello, Mr. Young," a voice from the reception area called when he reached the front door.

"Danielle, you startled me. You weren't here when I came in."

"They sent me for a doughnut and bagel run." She rolled her eyes. "Next time, I told them to place the order early and have it delivered."

"Exactly. It's not in your job description." Chase smiled. "But, thanks for doing it." He reached for his wallet and pulled out a fifty. "Don't do it again. And, if they ask why, have them call me."

Danielle broke into a smile. "I will. Thanks." She touched his hand. "But I don't need this."

Chase laid it in front of her. "I insist."

"Are you leaving, or will you be here for a while?"

"I'll walk the grounds then leave. Take a message if someone wants me. Don't find me."

"Okay, whatever you say, boss. Should I send everything Bobbie's way?"

"Yes." Chase pushed the front door open and stepped out into a humid, overcast day. "Looks like rain." He sent a smile Danielle's way and let the door go behind him.

Chase walked away from the buildings and toward the landing strip. Watching planes take off and land had a calming effect on him. He was away from prying ears and eyes, too, and could safely call Smith.

"Hello, Mr. Young." Smith answered on the first ring. "Before you say anything or go off on one of your tirades, hear me out. My people thought you should be made aware of your father's situation. Yes, I tipped him off where to find you. Regardless of the outcome, I thought you'd want to know. You're a good man, Chase."

Chase. He called me Chase. His temper which had flared to a boil as he made the call had diffused to a simmer. "You're right. I'd want to know. But, from now on, stay out of my personal business."

"I will."

"Wait! One more personal question. You never answered if Grace was in danger."

"Danger is a strong word, Mr. Young. I believe she is in peril."

"Physically?"

"I hope not."

"You hope or you know?" Chase's blood shot through his veins at record speed. "Smith, I want my phone back *now*. Do you hear me? Smith? Damn." He held back from throwing the phone on the walkway, his only link to Grace. *Grace! She needs to see the picture I took.*

The sky rumbled with thunder and Chase jogged to his car. Rain hit the hood as soon as he started the engine. He sent her a text to meet at her condo and put the Honda into reverse. It made a strange noise, but he brushed it off, blaming himself for being in a hurry. Raindrops pelted the car harder when he reached the highway. A bolt of lightning lit up the sky as if someone had turned on the lights in the darkened day, giving him enough time to catch sight of another car skidding across the lanes, headed straight for him.

Having front wheel drive, Chase held the brakes down and the wheel steady. "The crazy maniac must be going over the speed limit and when the storm hit couldn't slow down in time. "What the…"

The Honda didn't slow and kept going the same speed. Due to his driving skills, Chase managed not to collide with the skidding car, but now, his was out of control. Construction lights distracted him, flashing a giant arrow to move to the left. He had nowhere to go with traffic bumper to bumper on his driver's side. The passenger side front end hit an orange barrel then another. *Shit, no!*

The last thing Chase saw was a concrete barrier.

* * * *

When he opened his eyes, Grace smiled down on him. "Angel?" he whispered.

"No, it's me, Grace. You didn't die." Her face changed to a serious look for a quick second then returned to smiling. "You'll be fine."

Chase felt his hand in hers. "How did you …?"

"You only had a driver's license and the Falcon ID on you. They called Paul, and he told me. We're both here."

To check if I'm dead, I'm sure. "The car?"

"Totaled."

"I want it. Don't let it get taken to a junkyard."

"Okay. Don't worry about it. I'm sure your insurance company will handle the details."

Chase scanned his body with his eyes for any casts on limbs, burns or surgery scars. "What's my diagnosis?"

"For starters, a terrible concussion. There's a large gash on your forehead that took ten stitches to close. Thankfully, it's in the hairline. The doctor said you're lucky. It could have been much worse. Thank goodness for airbags, right? Paul says you won't be flying this week and I agree."

"Grace? My phone?"

"That's right. You texted me you had something you wanted to show me." Grace opened the bag of Chase's belongings. "Not in here."

"It's proof of who's behind…"

Paul walked into the room. "Chase, good to see you're awake."

"I'm in a room already?"

"It's been quite a few hours, Chase. In fact, it's almost midnight." Paul answered. "They're keeping you for observation. I told them you're one of my pilots and I need you cleared before you fly again." He touched his daughter's shoulder. "We should all get some sleep. You can visit in the morning, Gracie. Take the day off tomorrow."

"Thanks, Dad." Grace put her hand over his. "Could you give us a minute?"

"Sure, I'll be in the hall." Paul strolled out the door.

"Are you thinking what I am?" Grace squeezed Chase's hand.

"That I don't want you to leave?" He winced as he tried to smile.

"Yes, that, but we need to find your phone."

"Before you come tomorrow, see if you can find out where they took the car," Chase said in a low voice, hoping Paul couldn't hear. "I'm positive it's in the car, but don't go without me. When I'm released, we'll head straight there."

"*If* they release you, otherwise I'll go myself."

"No! Didn't you hear me? Don't go without me."

Grace kissed his cheek. "Get some rest. I'll be back in the morning."

Chase watched her leave, wishing she could stay, yet he needed time to think. "Craig, you bastard. You're probably watching the local news or waiting for a call that Chase Young is in serious condition or dead. My alias has worked in my favor." He tried to go over the events of the day even as a hammer pounded in his head. *Did I tip my hand? Craig got suspicious when I asked if he was happy. After our talk, he didn't leave the building and watched where I went. While in the field, he did something to the brakes of the Honda.*

"How did he know the Honda was mine?" Chase lightly touched the bandage on his forehead. "Andy probably told him. That's why Craig came over to the office." He wanted to put a call into the Society, get their opinions. Knowing Nash, he'd suggest a beatdown would be in order. "I should press charges, but I have no proof."

* * * *

Grace sat in her car and cried. She'd almost lost someone she loved today. *Love?*

At first, her dad felt the accident was intentional, someone going after his pilots. After a long discussion though, he thought differently. How could someone know Chase was in that car unless someone followed him? Grace argued it could have happened, her dad blamed the weather. She'd never seen him that way before, crushed and defeated. He would have fought with everything he had to find the truth. The pressure of the past months had taken their toll.

After the crazy day at the office, where she and her dad argued over the fate of the company, Paul got the call about Chase. She didn't have the heart to tell Chase what happened earlier, Paul was thinking of stepping down as CEO and dividing his shares among his children. They'd still be a majority, but it'd be three deciding, not one. She wasn't ready for it and neither were her brothers although they'd disagree.

Grace had also discovered someone was buying up large portions of their stock. Soon, they could be on equal footing with the shareholder if not careful. She had to convince her dad not to divide his stock. One of her brothers might sell some for financial gain, the other to support his family. Her dad was unaware of how her brothers felt about the company. She considered it a legacy, and they did not.

The rain had stopped hours ago, leaving a clean, fresh smell in the air. Grace let her window down and drove home breathing the night air. She planned to rise early, find Chase's car and get his phone.

Once home, Grace forced herself to go to bed. She tossed and turned, sleeping an hour or two here and there. When the first light of day came through the edges of the shaded window, she got up and showered. "Coffee. I need coffee." She started a pot and flipped through her phone, looking for a contact. "The police! They'd tell me where the car was taken."

The police finally gave the address of the impound lot after she'd convinced them she was Chase's sister, and he couldn't talk on the phone. *Keep using that excuse, Gracie girl! You're making a fine detective.*

The next call led her to a dead end. Yes, the car was at the lot, but they would not release it to anyone except the owner. It included visiting the car and checking for belongings. "Darn!" Grace pounded the table. She wanted to spare Chase the trip, get the phone and arrange for someone to check the car. "Someone tampered with Chase's brakes. I know it."

But what if whoever did it has the same idea? Get to the car before Chase and check for evidence? "I need to get there first, break in if all else fails. I can't do this by myself and know just the person to call for help."

CHAPTER FOURTEEN

Grace glanced at her phone. *Six-thirty*. She didn't wait to call. Darcy might be going to the diner. "Come on, Darcy, pick up!"

"Hey, who's calling me so early on my day off. This better be good."

"That's wonderful!"

"What is?" Darcy huffed into the phone. "Grace, girl, start from the beginning. Why did you call me so early?"

After Grace told her story, Darcy shouted, "I'm in!" and promised to be waiting at the front door of the apartment. Grace found her leaning against the wall when she pulled to the curb, dressed in a black-t-shirt, black tight jeans and running shoes. She'd pulled her lavender tinted hair into a short ponytail.

"I have a plan," Darcy said as she slid into the passenger side. "You're the distraction. I hop the fence."

"We don't know if it's that easy, Darcy. It could have barbed wire around the top."

"Did you set your GPS?"

"Yes, I did."

Darcy checked the location. "Looks like we can drive around the block, case the area before we go in." She sat back and looked at Grace. "How is Perfect? You didn't say."

"He'll have a bad headache for a few days, but the doctors say he's lucky. Besides the airbag, he protected his body well."

"Makes sense." Darcy chuckled. "He didn't want to damage the merchandise."

"Darcy!" Grace had to laugh with her. "He has a gash in his forehead that will probably leave a scar."

"Oh, no!" Darcy slapped the console.

"It's right at the hairline. It won't show."

"I'm glad we can kid about this, Grace. When you said you think someone did this to him, it gave me chills. Let's get the bastard."

"Or bastards."

"I hope we beat them to the car." Darcy rubbed her hands together. "You never told me working at Falcon could be this much fun."

Grace glanced at her from the corner of her eye. "You're taking the offer?"

"On one condition." Darcy let out a breath. "Only if you agree to still let me work there if I don't get the scholarship."

"You will get it, but even if you don't, you have a job."

"My mom said you wouldn't agree."

"Your mom doesn't know me." Grace reached over and patted Darcy's hand. "We're almost there." She checked the time. "They opened at six a.m. Maybe we can find a way in without jumping a fence."

"I know this sounds lame, but whoever you talk to, you've got to act sweet and innocent. Are you still going to say you're Perfect's sister? Take your time explaining why you need to get to the car. I'll find a way in."

"Sounds like you've done this before." Grace guided the car around the block and into the parking lot. Once parked, she stared at Darcy. "Well? Have you?"

"Maybe?" Darcy shrugged.

A line had formed at the entrance and a chain-link fence blocked anyone from going in or out. The guard pointed to a special gate and pushed a button if he let someone into the lot. A larger gate for cars was on the other side of the booth.

"We may have lucked out," Darcy whispered to Grace as they got in line.

A tow truck with an SUV attached to its hook pulled up to the gate. Darcy dashed to the back end of the car and it was the last Grace saw of her as the gate slowly opened.

"May I help you?" The man behind the plexiglass looked tired and bored. Grace hoped he didn't wave her off too quickly.

"My brother's car is here."

"License and registration."

"His or mine?" Grace blinked.

"His, and an ID to prove you're his sister."

"You mean I can go to the car if I have those documents?"

"All depends."

"On?"

"The car, the owner and what you're looking for."

"Oh! That's easy. He left his cell in the car and needs it for business."

"Why doesn't he come himself?"

"Chase is still in the hospital recovering from the crash. He has a nasty concussion and can't drive or walk well."

"That is sad." The man rubbed his chin. "I'm sorry I can't let you in."

"You have to let me in." Grace tried to appear distraught. *If I could get in there, two of us are better than one.* "Please?"

Grace heard grumblings behind her and glanced over her shoulder. The line had grown longer with impatient people. She needed to stall for time. "Um."

"Grace!" Darcy called to her, letting herself out through the special gate. "What are you doing here?"

"Thanks for your help." Grace made a face at the man and stepped away from the window.

"Walk with me," Darcy whispered. "Not too fast and head for the parking lot."

"Did you get it?"

Darcy didn't say another word until they were in the car. "Lock the doors." She presented the phone like she'd found a hidden treasure. "We need to know if the damn thing still works." She checked for the power tab.

"No." Grace placed her hand over Darcy's and the phone. "We'll take it to the hospital and let Chase do it."

"Fair enough." Darcy slid it in her pocket and looked out the window. "Let's get out of here. This place gives me the creeps. Too many dead cars in there."

"Chase will be surprised to see you, "Grace said once they were on the road.

"He will kill us both when he finds out what we did."

"Maybe at first. There was no way he could have gone to the lot today, Darcy. I don't think he realizes how bad this concussion is. He was unconscious for hours, had an MRI and didn't even know it."

"Do you think they'll release him today?"

"Knowing Chase, he'll fight to go home." Grace smiled, picturing him charming the nurses into saying he was fine. "Tell the doctor for me," he would say.

The hospital parking garage came into view, and Grace had to drive up a few levels before she found a space. Darcy followed her to Chase's room where they found him eating breakfast. His eyes lit up when he saw them.

"My two favorite girls," Chase said with a wink.

"Oh, Perfect." Darcy held up a hand. "A hospital gown and a huge gauze bandage on your head, not quite your look."

"And here, I thought you'd like it." Chase patted the edge of the bed. "Sit."

Darcy gave Grace a push toward the bed as she slumped into a chair. Grace took Chase's hand as she slid onto the mattress. "How are you feeling?"

"I'm going home this afternoon." He grinned. "That's if you're willing to take me."

"*If* the doctors say you can leave." Grace squeezed his hand. "I didn't get much sleep last night. I kept thinking about your phone and decided it had to be in the car."

"That's the first place I want you take me."

Darcy cleared her throat and Chase glanced her way. "Yes, Darcy?" He lifted his brows and looked back at Grace. "No…you didn't."

Grace nodded. "We have your phone, and I give all the credit to Darcy. The girl's a ninja." She looked at Darcy and they laughed.

"If I didn't have such a headache, I'd let you two have it. What you did was dangerous. Someone else may want that phone."

"That's why we got it, Perfect. Grace had a good plan."

"Who has it?" Chase looked from one woman to the other.

Darcy dug in her pocket and produced the evidence. "I do. We didn't test to see if it worked.

Grace said you should be the one." She leaned forward and gave the cell to Grace.

"Here." Grace prayed the phone turned on and the picture was still there. She held her breath until the device came to life.

Chase scrolled through a few screens and she watched his face for clues. He nodded as he handed her the phone. "This was on Craig's desk. The name Edison with a number beneath it. Do you recognize who it belongs to?"

Grace tried to keep her hand from shaking as her body trembled. The number jumped out at her, causing her stomach to flip. "It's not my dad's number, Chase. It's Mark's."

* * * *

Chase had hoped none of Grace's family was involved. His heart ached for her. The pain on her face made him want to gather her up in his arms and never let go. "I'm sorry, baby." He glanced at Darcy to make sure she wasn't about to make a snide comment. Instead, he saw tears in her eyes.

"What are we going to do, Perfect?"

"We will not jump to conclusions, Darcy. I happened to get lucky, spot the guy hanging around the airport talking with Mark and followed him to his place of work. I thought he didn't notice me, but I guess I'm not a great detective."

"You think he let you break into his office?" Darcy asked. "Meanwhile, someone was slashing your brake line."

Chase winced. "Maybe." He was getting in over his head with lies but couldn't tell the truth.

"My brother may have tried to run you off the road after someone tampered with your brakes! That guy might have called him after you left." Grace covered her mouth and tears rolled down her cheeks.

"For now, it's safe to say the skidding car might been anyone." *Craig is more desperate than Mark. He knew I was close or had figured out what he was doing. Damn! He didn't care if he killed me. I thought I knew the man.* Chase tugged on Grace's hand. "I don't understand why Mark went about it this way, but now we know he's the one working with the blonde man Candance mentioned."

"I have some idea why he had to," Grace answered. "Few would sell their stock if the company's doing well. What's the saying? Buy low. Sell high. Mark needed the stock to drop so his friend could buy low."

"His friend's name," Chase interrupted. "was on his door. Craig Hawk."

"Ok, we have a name. That's a start. With Mark's shares, Craig bought enough so they could be majority shareholders." She shook her head. "I don't understand what Mark gets out of this. He'd eventually own the company."

"With you and your brother," Chase said. "This way he'd have one partner, and we don't know what Craig promised him."

"I need to talk to him, Chase. Hear his side of the story."

"Not without me."

"Or me." Darcy waved from her seat. "Hey, Chase, guess what?"

"Really, Darcy?"

"Yeah, really. I plan to quit the diner tomorrow. Tell them it's last shift."

"She'll work for me either way, scholarship or not." Grace tried to lift the corners of her mouth.

Chase touched her cheek. "How did I get so lucky to find you?"

"I'm the lucky one." Grace came close and brushed his lips with hers. "Tell me if anything hurts."

"That's what I needed."

"Can you two lovebirds get back to the subject of grilling Mark and finding this asshole Craig?" Darcy asked. "Where's the fricking doctor when you need him?"

"I told you," Chase said. "They're releasing me this afternoon if I have a driver. Look at me. Good as new."

"I highly doubt that." Grace ran her hand down his arm. "I'm going to take good care of you."

"Mr. Garrett?" A nurse stood at the door. "I'm told you can leave as long as you go home and do nothing for forty-eight hours." She shook her head. "Be very careful. If anything makes you dizzy, stop doing it. I suggest no cell phones or TV today."

"I'll make sure," Grace answered for him. She looked at Darcy. "Looks like our plans are on hold. Work your shift tomorrow then come to my house early on Friday. Chase and I should have figured out something by then."

Even though he fought staying with Grace, not wanting her to wait on him, Chase caved and let her take him to the condo. He ended up sleeping the rest of the day and most of the next, admonishing himself every time he woke. By Thursday evening, he was stir-crazy and convinced Grace to walk outside instead of around the rooms of her condo.

"I'm much better." Chase kissed the side of her head. "I feel bad you took off work. I can stay here on my own."

"I wanted to be here, Chase." Grace tucked her arm through his. "I love … taking care of you."

They'd been doing that for the past two days, start a sentence with "I love" and finishing with a random comment. Chase wanted to end the game they played with the real statement, but after what happened to him and Grace's tragedy with Sean, he hesitated. "And I love … the idea of taking you to bed tonight and not sleeping."

"Are you sure?" Grace paused by the pool entrance. "Want to sit?"

Chase hadn't been back since their pool encounter. He longed to tell Grace he had a private pool where they could swim and make love whenever she wanted. "Okay."

"Tell me if the waterfall bothers you."

"It will be a good test." Chase noticed the place was empty and pulled Grace into a smoldering kiss. He ran his hands into her silky hair, tugging lightly. "I want you to be mine," he murmured between kisses. "Say you will."

"I will."

Chase felt Grace's body almost go limp in his arms, pressing her body against his. A chaise was nearby, and he lowered them onto the cushion. Grace snuggled against him. "I don't want to spoil the mood, but I need to go to the office tomorrow, for at least an hour."

Chase tensed. "No."

"Mark has a late flight to New York City tonight. He won't be back until tomorrow afternoon."

"Who's in the building that early?"

"No one. I lock the door."

"Not a good idea."

"What if I have Darcy with me? She can fill out application forms while I work."

"If you keep me on speaker phone the whole time, I might agree."

"Okay." Grace kissed the tip of his nose. "If it makes you happy. Let's get you back to the house."

The walk did him good, and Chase enjoyed dinner on the patio with Grace then an early bedtime. She helped him undress, did the same and slid into bed, slowly lowering herself next to him. "Are you sure?"

"Yes." He breathed in her scent, kissing her neck and rolling her onto her back. Chase looked into her eyes. "I know this is too soon." He paused. "I love you."

"I love you, too. Let me show you how much."

* * * *

Grace was out the door at seven-thirty, planning to meet Darcy at Falcon before eight. Chase made excuses to keep her from leaving before then. Paul usually checked in by seven-thirty. "Call me as soon as you get there." Chase reminded her. She'd been gone fifteen minutes when the doorbell rang. "Did you forget something?" Chase threw the door back to find a messenger on the small porch.

"Mr. Young?"

"Yes." Chase wrinkled his brow.

"I have a package for you." He handed him a padded envelope. "Have a good day."

"Wait…" Chase wanted to tip the guy, but he seemed in a hurry. He examined the outside, finding no return address or postage marks, just his name.

A steaming mug of coffee sat on the counter, and Chase grabbed it on his way to the great room to settle in on the sofa. He tugged on the pull-tab of the envelope and shook the contents onto the cushion next to him. His phone bounced onto the couch, the last thing he expected to see. "Does this mean my assignment's done?"

Chase leaned back to think, finally able to focus on the last few days. The morning after the accident, he'd used the hospital phone to call his security people and given strict orders to watch Craig constantly and not to let him leave the city. If he filed a flight plan, it was to be denied. Only approach and detain, if necessary, he instructed. Chase wanted to be the one to confront him. He told them to bring up all C. Y. footage from Tuesday and send it to Bobbie. *What was Craig thinking? He didn't know the parking lot had cameras?* "Unless he erased it."

The second call had been to the impound lot. Under no circumstances should anyone be allowed to go to his car while under their care. He threatened a lawsuit if anything was missing from the Honda. Chase had a strange feeling Grace would try to go there without him and wanted to stop her. If she couldn't get in she'd have no evidence to put her in danger, or peril, as Mr. Smith had stated.

"Smith!" Chase fumbled for the burner phone and made the call.

"Mr. Young, are you feeling better?"

"Yes, I am. I got my phone back. Does that mean I'm done with the assignment?"

"You have a few loose ends, but yes, you have saved Falcon. Your friend? I do not know what you plan to do about him."

"Craig? He's not really a friend…" Chase scratched at his jaw. "I guess he was, but he needs to sit on his ass in a jail cell for a while."

"That is one recourse."

"What do you mean that is *one* recourse? The man tried to kill me!"

"Perhaps. Desperate times lead to desperate measures."

Chase grimaced. "True. Why is Craig so desperate, Smith? Can you tell me that? I'm sure you know."

"He and Mark Edison are alike in many ways. They feel overlooked by the powers that be. They want to be the top dog, run things their way, although they may find it's not always so glorious at the top, am I right?"

"For once, we agree. Here's the burning question. Why go to such lengths to get the company? Mark's already in and Craig could continue to buy shares until he had what he wanted. Do it the right way."

"Ah, but there's the problem. Craig had found a partner but with the wrong airline. Falcon is doing well. His only recourse was to tank the stock. I don't approve of his methods, but I feel he got in over his head and couldn't stop."

"So, we forgive him?" Chase wanted to run his hand through his hair, but a headache and bandage stopped him.

"I feel charges are in order, Mr. Young. Only you can decide what they should be."

"Again, we play the game," Chase said through gritted teeth. "I feel I did my job, and we are done. I can tell Grace who I am now."

"Not yet, I'm afraid. We have five more Society members to go. Grace cannot know any details until they are done."

"She'd never jeopardize the mission."

"You are correct. But, once you tell someone a secret, you can never take it back."

"I can't believe I'm going to say this again. You're right. I don't like it, but I'll figure out something. Now, what about Darcy? Will she get the scholarship?"

"Will she do the work and fill out the application?"

"Yes, Grace and I will make sure."

"Then, yes, she will."

"You know I could fund her education."

"Would she want you to?"

"Probably not." Chase let out a breath. "How long before I can see Grace again?"

"Six weeks."

"What? That's a long time. Why six weeks, Smith?" Chase looked at the screen. "Call ended! Damn that man!"

Tempted to throw the phone, he slipped it back into his pocket before he did. Chase hoped someone kept his cell charged and hit the button. The screen came to life, bombarding him with text and phone messages. He ignored most and scrolled to the most recent. The last one caught his attention being in all caps, "CALL ME".

CHAPTER FIFTEEN

"Bobbie!" Chase dialed her office phone, and she picked up on the second ring.

"Oh, thank the Lord, you have a working phone again."

"Bobbie, is everything all right?"

"Yes, I got a message from your daddy's doctor. They would not leave a message or give me any information. They will only talk to you. I'm sending you the number now." Bobbie paused. "Where have you been, Sugar?"

"I was in a car accident Tuesday."

"Oh, my heavens, no! Why didn't you call me or your mama? She'd have driven all night to get here!"

"I'm fine. I had a concussion and had to stay overnight for observation."

"Then come home. I can call Maureen, and she'll be here in six hours."

After the divorce, Maureen had landed a job at the same company where Allan Rivers worked. Over time, their friendship turned to love, encouraged by Bobbie along the way. After they married, they bought a house in the suburbs. Chase lived there until he left for college. During his freshman year, Red was offered a great job in St. Augustine, Florida. It had been a good time to move. Ella would enter middle school and could make new friends although she resisted the idea. Chase knew she'd be fine even as she texted him poop emojis for the first week there.

"Please, don't call my mom. I'm fine. I'll tell her when I have time. Right now, I'm caught up in the middle of something."

"All right, but don't ask me to lie when she asks how you are."

"Never." Chase smiled. "I will call the doctor and text you the details."

"Thank you. I hope it's good news."

Chase opened his texts after they ended the call, found the number and called the doctor's office. After giving his name, the receptionist put him on hold.

"Chase Young?" A woman's voice answered.

"Yes."

"I am Doctor Scofield's nurse. I can answer any questions you have."

"What's wrong with my dad?"

"He doesn't have Parkinson's, if that's what worries you. Mr. Young has what we call hand tremors. It isn't life-threatening but can make daily tasks difficult. It's a common neurological disorder, but we don't know what causes it."

"Is there anything that can be done?"

"There is medication."

"Was my father prescribed medicine?"

"He will be when he comes in today."

"Is there anything we can do for it? To stop it?"

"I'm afraid not, but the good news is the doctor can treat him and nothing else should come of it."

"Thank you. My assistant told you where to send the bills?"

"Yes, she took care of everything."

"And Nurse …?"

"Sheila. Sheila Grey."

"Sheila, take good care of him."

"We certainly will."

Chase's back pocket vibrated. "Grace!" He'd almost forgotten being caught up in the other calls. "Baby?"

"I'm here with Darcy and Dad is in his office. No dead falcons to speak of." Grace joked, but Chase heard the nerves in her voice.

"I shouldn't have let you go there alone."

"I'm not alone, plus I learned Mark is flying back from New York City and should be back by two. I asked Dad to bring him to the office after he lands. He needs to hear everything."

"Since I don't have a car, someone needs to come and get me. I'm not hanging out here alone until… what time do you think he'll get to Falcon, three o'clock?"

"I'll get him, Grace."

Chase smiled, glad Grace put the phone on speaker. "I'll be waiting, Darcy. Tell Grace we'll bring lunch."

After ending the call, Chase hurried to get ready, pocketing both phones and wallet. He'd thought about Craig and what he would love to do to him. "Maybe he's put it all together by now. Craig thought he was stopping me, Chase Young, from interfering with his plan. But, if he heard from Mark, he'd figure out pretty fast, I was flying for Falcon. Let's hope you've been on radio silence, Marky boy."

Knowing Darcy, she'd be here in less than fifteen minutes to get him. He'd wait for her on the small front porch where Grace had set two white wicker chairs.

Chase didn't sit long, Darcy maneuvered her car up to the curb, rolled the passenger side window down and yelled, "Get in, Perfect!"

* * * *

Grace's office phone rang, startling her back to reality. She couldn't wrap her mind around work and had sat staring at her computer screen after Darcy left. "Grace Edison," she answered.

"Have you had enough?" An unfamiliar man's voice asked.

"I have no idea what you're talking about. Who is this?"

"A friend."

"I don't think so."

"I will be once I save your company."

Her heart skipped a beat. *It's him!* "The company doesn't need saving."

"It might, and being a minority stockholder soon to be majority, you owe it to me to listen."

Minority stockholder becoming a majority one? Grace quickly did the numbers in her head. Her dad had given each of them enough of the company combined with his percent before going public to always be the majority shareholders. Paul's plan was for each child to receive more at his retirement, so they'd always be in control. No way could he reach majority status unless he teamed up with someone.

If her brother Mark joined forces with someone able to buy the percent needed in the public sector, they'd have power over her dad. Grace's mind spun with different outcomes. "Why don't you make an appointment, and we can talk?"

"Oh, I didn't call to ask your permission or make an appointment. This is a courtesy call. When you meet me, I'll be your new boss."

Grace slammed the phone down in its holder. "No effing way!"

"Whoa, is my girl an almost swearer?"

Grace looked up into Chase's smiling eyes. "Yes … I guess … that was the mysterious man who's been buying up shares of the company."

Chase sat down across from her. "The bastard called you?"

"Yes, to tell me the next time we meet, I'll be calling him boss."

"No, you won't."

Grace studied Chase's guarded expression. "Is there something you're not telling me? I feel you left something out from the accident. Where was your car parked that this guy had access to it and knew it belonged to you?"

"A case of bad luck?" Chase scratched his jaw, but Grace said nothing. "Darcy's got lunch. She wouldn't let me carry a thing."

Nice 'time to change the subject again' move. Her brothers thought they were the experts, but Grace was the champion. She recognized a smooth change and gave him props. *I'll get it out of him later.*

Chase pointed his thumb over his shoulder. "When did the real falcon arrive? I saw it on its perch in the foyer."

"It was Fed Ex'ed over after Dad called them." Grace rolled her eyes. "After what happened, he still put it on display."

After lunch, Paul appeared in the doorway as requested. "I did what you asked, Grace, now care to update me?"

"Come in, Dad." Grace looked at Chase. "I don't know how to start." *How do I tell my dad one of his sons thought nothing of sabotaging his company?*

"Do you want me to …?" Chase lifted his shoulders.

"Please."

Chase cleared his throat. "Paul, we need to speak to Mark about the strange incidents that have occurred at Falcon."

"You think he has information?" Paul asked.

"Yes, but we feel he has been led astray by someone else."

"Someone's using my boy to sabotage Falcon?"

'Not exactly."

"Oh, for goodness' sake!" Grace huffed. "We think he's in on it, Dad."

"What?" Paul rubbed his face. "No! I can't believe it."

"That's why we want to talk to him, Paul," Chase added.

"And, I shouldn't be here," Darcy said as she rose from her chair. "It's almost three. I'm going to make myself scarce. You know how to find me."

Paul stared at Grace. "Please tell me this is a joke."

"I wish I could. I'd like to hear Mark's side of the story before we accuse him of anything major."

Paul swung his head in Chase's direction. "Why does he have to be here?"

"He's been in on it from the beginning. And besides, we owe him. Someone tried to kill him."

"Kill is a strong word," Chase said.

Grace gave him a hard stare. "In your opinion, what *was* he trying to do?"

"Get me out of the way? Send a warning as to what could happen to your pilots? They'd quit in droves if they heard what happened to me."

"Thanks for keeping it to yourself, Chase." Paul nodded. "At least, till we work things out."

"I never thought of the impact it would have on the other pilots." Grace pounded her desk. "This stops now."

"What does?" Mark stood in his pilot's uniform at the door.

"Come in, Mark. Take a seat." She gestured to where Darcy had been sitting. Her heart pounded so loudly it bounced off her eardrums. She took a few breaths to calm herself. "We know you are helping sabotage Falcon."

"Bullshit!" Mark stood to leave but Chase hopped up to block him.

"Chase!" Grace didn't want to worry about him, too. "Please, don't."

"Sit. Down," Chase said through gritted teeth.

"All right." Mark held up his hands. He looked at Grace with pleading eyes. "Hear me out?"

"You start and if I like what I hear, I'll let you finish." Grace folded her arms across her chest.

"I met Craig Hawk at a shareholder's meeting at the end of the year. Dad was sick, and I filled in for him. Remember?"

Grace stared at him, unable to speak.

"Craig introduced himself and said he had a proposal. I've heard many before, so I agreed thinking I'd let him down gently after we talked. He said he liked what he saw in me and thought I had potential. It wasn't the time or place to have a conversation. We agreed to have dinner in the new year. That's when Craig told me his plan. He'd buy up shares, we'd combine assets and he'd put me in charge of running the company. CEO. Full control. We'd change the name …"

"Let me guess," Grace interrupted. "Hawk Airlines."

"Yeah." Mark chuckled. "Falcon to hawk."

"Not funny, Mark." Grace's eyes landed on the watch. "And he gave you that?"

Mark glanced down at the timepiece. "The Seamaster? Yes, he did, as a token of our partnership."

"A watch? That's all it took? Gosh, Mark, it didn't take much to sway you to the dark side." Grace balled her hands into fists.

"Give me a break, Gracie. I was helping Dad."

"What?" Paul shifted and sat straighter in his seat. "How?"

"Craig has these great ideas, Dad. He works for a private airline and has tons of experience. He can envision the future of aviation and how to grow the company. Isn't that what you want?"

"I'm pretty happy with the way things are, Mark."

"When it's time to hand things over to your kids, it may not be." Mark looked from Grace to their dad and back again. "Craig's idea to have the stock drop was a good one. It seemed harmless to me and would help us get what we needed. He'd buy up the shares and I'd work on the inside making sure little things went wrong or switching numbers in the books to make it look like we were in the red."

"What?" Grace slammed her hand down. "How did you get into my computer?"

"I didn't have to, Sis. I changed numbers before I sent the reports to you." Mark glanced around the room. "Then suddenly, I don't know …" He shrugged. "Things got out of control. I had no idea Craig loosened the seats on the 737 or would send a dead falcon here. I was in over my head by then and didn't have a way out. I told him to stop. We were in a good place."

"You knew he put people's lives in danger and did nothing?" Grace felt the heat creep up her neck.

"No! Only after the fact, I did. I called him on it every time."

"That was big of you." Grace rolled her eyes.

"Your father has every right to have you arrested, Mark," Chase said. "He could press charges."

"Go ahead. He doesn't care about me," Mark scoffed.

"Mark! How can you say that?" Paul yelled.

"Well, do you care, Dad? Do you ever listen to my ideas? No. Did I ever get the flights I wanted? No. Is Tim your golden boy? Yes. Don't tell me he isn't heir apparent to Falcon. Gracie's happy in her role and Tim always checks in with her. Me? I might as well be invisible. Craig saw me for who I am and what I can achieve. He has faith in me."

"I do, too, son."

"No, Dad, you don't. I could really make something of this place if you'd let me. But, no, go sit over there in the corner, Mark, and do what I say. I never planned to tank the company. It was the opposite. I did it *for* you, Dad." Mark swiped at his eyes. "I wanted you to see what I could do, make more money than you'd ever imagine."

"I don't care about the money, Mark."

"Don't say that, Dad. Everyone cares about money. If this hadn't taken off like you hoped, you'd be in bankruptcy court."

"You're right. What I meant to say is I hoped this would be a lasting legacy, one the Edisons would run for many years to come."

"I'm sorry." Mark locked eyes with Grace. "What can I do to make this better?"

"A real apology would help … to Dad, not me. I don't know if I could ever trust you again, Mark. I would like your airport security clearance and Falcon badge."

"Dad!" Mark spun in Paul's direction. "Are you going to let her get away with this?"

"Yes, son, I am. Give her the badges."

"I'll talk with Dad later," Grace said. "My recommendation will be termination. We'll give you an outstanding referral for any airline. Of course, you still have your shares in Falcon. Finally, call Craig Hawk and tell him the deal is off. If he wants to talk to someone, tell him to call your boss … me." Grace noticed her dad sitting with his head in his hands. "It has to be done this way, Dad. We can't ever trust him on Falcon property again."

Paul nodded but didn't look up.

"Well, Mark, you got your wish, Dad's full attention. Like what you've done to him? If I have my way, you won't be invited to Thanksgiving or Christmas this year and will need to grovel your way back into the family. At work, I may feel one way about you, but on a personal level, I can't cut you off. You'll need to give us time to adjust and accept what you've done. After that, prove who you really are to the family. Maybe one day we'll trust you again." Grace stood. "You're dismissed. Call your partner if you know what's good for you. Then, I want a list of everything you changed in the books. When you do those things, leave the property or I'll call the police."

Mark hung his head, his cocky attitude gone. "I'm sorry, Gracie. I'll make it up to you and everyone else. I promise."

Grace held her breath until he left the room. Her wildly beating heart had begun to slow as she rose from her desk. Paul still sat in the same position and she slid her arm around his back. "You okay, Dad? Everything's going to be fine. Mark's done stupid stuff all his life. He doesn't think, isn't that what you always say?"

Paul dropped his hands from his face. "This is different. I'm in shock right now and don't know what to say."

"Grace did a good job, Paul. It's the right thing to do. Craig used him, but Mark took things too far and you terminated him." Chase glanced out the window.

"What are you looking for, Chase?" Grace left her father's side to go to him.

"A car," he said under his breath.

"Did I hear you correctly? A car?" Grace placed her hands on her hips.

"I arranged for a rental. I have a few errands to run."

"Chase Garrett! Did the doctor clear you to drive?"

"He said if I had no symptoms, I could drive."

"You're making that up."

"Hey, I've been clearheaded since last night." Chase took her hand and kissed the top.

Grace glanced over her shoulder to check if her dad got the meaning. "Chase," she whispered. "Stop."

"I have your permission?" He lifted his dark brown eyes to meet hers, and she couldn't resist. "Fine, but call me every hour with updates on your health. If you feel faint or sick, I'll come and get you."

"Yes, ma'am. Meet you back at your place?" Chase hopped from the chair when he saw a car pull up to the building.

"Yes, I'll be there. I hope the reason you're leaving is important." Grace kissed him on the cheek although she longed to do more. "Take care."

CHAPTER SIXTEEN

Chase felt guilty lying to Grace, but he had to get away on his own. Some secrets had to be kept. The fact that he knew Craig Hawk was one of them. Knowing Craig like he did, he'd be at C.Y. acting as if nothing were wrong and feign innocence about Chase's accident.

A young man hopped from the rental car in front of the main entrance when Chase arrived. "Chase Garrett?"

"Yes, that's me." He gave the kid a twenty when he was handed the keys.

"Thanks!"

Another car pulled up and the young man ran to the passenger side. Chase had paid heavily for the car to be brought to him, but at least he now had his phone and access to his credit cards. Surprisingly, he'd asked for a Honda, and they brought him a CRV. He lifted his hand in a wave as he slid behind the wheel. His real phone rang, signaling Bobbie.

"Bobbie?"

"Hey, Sugar. I got the footage you had sent to me, but you're not going to like what I'm about to tell you."

"Go ahead. I know what you're going to say."

"There's no footage of you at C.Y., only black and white static."

"Can an expert take a look?" Chase touched his forehead. "You already had it checked."

"I did. Nothing could be retrieved. I have a feeling your accident wasn't really an accident, was it Chase?" Bobbie sounded concerned. "And you think someone at your own company did something to the car?"

Hearing it made his blood boil. "Something like that, yeah."

"Do you know who did it?"

"Yes."

"Then go get 'em." Bobbie, her mother bear coming out, made him chuckle. "What's so funny?"

"You, Bobbie. Do I ever thank you for all you do?"

"Every time I see you, Sugar. Don't you worry about a thing. Mama Bobbie's got your back." She paused. "You *are* going to tell me who did this."

"Soon, when the time is right. I've got to go." His hands began to shake as he started the car. He gripped the wheel tightly and clenched his jaw. "You can do this."

When the highway came into view, he swallowed and concentrated on the traffic. The scent of an unfamiliar car wore off and recognizing the Honda interior helped him settle in for the drive. If he could make it to C.Y. in one piece, Chase swore he'd go to the doctor.

Once on the highway, the humming of the car calmed him. Chase knew he had one thing going for him, the element of surprise. C.Y. Airlines was never called to tell them Chase Young was in an accident and Craig had no idea his alias was Chase Garrett. If Craig called hospitals to check if Chase Young was there, he'd be told no. Both sides, Falcon and Craig were clueless. He wanted to keep it that way.

Andy got out of his car in the airline parking lot as Chase pulled in. He shaded his eyes as if to see who'd get out of the SUV. "Got a thing for Hondas these days, boss?" He chuckled.

"I guess I do." Chase caught up with him. "Andy, I'd like to ask you a few questions."

"Sure."

"When I was here Tuesday, did you talk to Craig?"

"Yeah, he was in the flight school building when I arrived. I joked about the car you drove."

"Was he surprised I was here?"

"No." Andy shook his head. "He just said, 'I better get over to the main building and check if he needs any help.' Craig always says that. No different than any other time."

"Did he say anything else you can remember?"

Andy rubbed his chin. "I thought it strange at the time, but yes, he did."

Chase stared at him. "What was it?"

"He asked the color of your car. I said blue, he nodded and left."

"Where is he now?" Chase tried to keep a friendly tone. "Or did you just get here?"

"Just got here, but I'll call Danielle."

"Say you're checking on Craig. Don't mention me, I have a surprise for him." *A big one.*

Andy walked to a desk and picked up an office phone, returning in a minute. "He's in his office."

"Thanks, Andy. You're doing a great job here at the school. Need anything?"

"If I think of something, I'll let you know."

Chase saluted and strode to the door, holding back from an all-out run. He couldn't get to Craig's office quick enough. No one would recognize his car. Andy had no reason to tip him off. *Should I jump into his doorway, arms out and say I'm alive?*

"Hello, Mr. Young," Danielle said from behind the desk.

"Hi, Danielle. How are you today? No doughnut runs, I hope?"

"No." She laughed.

"Quitting time soon. Enjoy the weekend." Chase proceeded down the hall toward Craig's office. He could hear him talking as he drew nearer.

"What do you mean the deal is off? So what if they know? I'm close to getting those shares. Can you hang in there a few more weeks?"

Chase stepped into the doorway.

"Can I call you back? Something came up." Craig's face was priceless. Chase wished he had the nerve to take a picture. "Chase? You're…"

"Alive?" Chase took a step into the office.

Craig rolled back in his chair away from the desk, holding up his hands. "I don't know what you're talking about."

"A shame about the security camera, isn't it? We need to call the company and complain."

"I didn't know there was a problem."

You're good, Craig, but I'm better. I'm about to call your bluff." Chase made his hands into fists to keep him from scratching his jaw. "I don't know if you're aware, but I was in a car accident on Tuesday, right after I left here."

To Chase's surprise, Craig managed to show a real look of shock and concern.

"I had the footage from our parking lot sent to a lab that specializes in retrieving film because the film *was* messed up."

"That's too bad. Wonder what happened?" Craig appeared relieved.

"I guess you didn't hear me. I said the footage *was* all static before I sent it … as in past tense."

"Oh?" Craig slowly got up from his seat and walked to the edge of his desk.

"Looking for an escape?" Chase lifted his brows.

"No. You're standing so I thought I would."

"What did you do to the brakes, Craig?"

"Chase, you're talking in circles. I have no idea what you're saying. You're going on about parking lots, footage, static and never got to the point."

"Then let me start from the beginning. Andy told you I drove the blue Honda here on Tuesday. I had a car accident and totaled the car. Funny, the brakes didn't seem to work. When I requested the footage from our parking lot, it was all static...but, not anymore." Chase folded his arms and stared at Craig. "Don't make me say it, Craig. Or do you want to tell the police what went down?"

"Dammit, shit," Craig said almost to himself. "I didn't want you to get hurt, Chase. I needed you out of the way until I finished what I started. I was afraid you'd drive straight to Falcon and report me."

Chase patted his pocket, hoping the phone picked up every word. "You admit you did something to my brakes to stop me from what? Tattling on you?"

"If you want to put it that way, I guess so," Craig scoffed. "Cut it out, Chase. You figured out I was buying stock to become a majority shareholder in Falcon. Maybe I didn't go about it in a completely legit way, but there's no proof."

"Okay, I'll admit I have no proof about the shares but what about tampering with my car? You can get jail time for that."

"I'll claim I was checking the car for safety reasons. Look, Chase, you're young. I'm in my mid-forties. This is your company. I've worked for you for five years and want more. My own airline. Is that so bad?"

"The way you went about it was. I have a feeling the deal's off."

"You heard." Craig smirked. "Mark's a pussy. I thought he had more balls, wanting it bad enough to do anything it took."

"You crossed a line, Craig. The loose seats were the tip of the iceberg."

"That's all they were, Chase! Hey. How did you know about that?"

"I flew that plane to Miami."

"You work for Falcon?"

"No, I was doing a friend a favor. Thank God, I did. I would've never found out about you. I discovered you're loyal as shit, Craig. I trusted you with my company. Didn't think I had to micromanage you. What an idiot, I was!"

"You weren't. You could trust me. I don't know what came over me. The Falcon stock was available, and something clicked in my head. I couldn't sleep or eat. All I could think about was ways to get my own airline. Come on, Chase. You know how it is." Craig appeared to be inching toward the door.

"I don't." Chase stared at him, daring him to move one more step. "Desperate measures." He shook his head. "You know what's funny?"

Craig looked at him with questioning eyes. "No, what?"

"I would've helped you start your own airline or buy into one if you'd asked. You son of a bitch, you didn't trust me enough to tell me."

"I thought you'd fight to keep me."

"I would have! Isn't that a compliment to your talents? Once I thought about it, I would have been on your side. I never thought you had it in you to do some of the things you've done. You sent a dead bird to Falcon!"

"What are you going to do?"

"At first, I wanted to call the police, throw the book at you. But you're right. I have no real evidence to back up my claim. Mark told all, but it's your word against his."

"Wait a minute." Craig shook his pointer finger. "What about the security camera. You said you saw the footage."

"I told you I saw static. I never said they fixed it or pulled any images from the film."

"Why you…" Craig lunged for him.

Chase's head still pounded from the concussion, but he was up for the challenge. Craig pushed him backward, setting him off-balance and his brain spinning. Chase fought to gain control of his senses, needing to stop Craig before he got out the door. He dropped a shoulder, planted it in Craig's gut and heard a whoosh of air come from him. Craig worked out but not to the extent Chase did. Even in his weakened condition, Chase thought he could take him. The struggle seemed to last forever, yet Chase knew it was a matter of minutes. He had to go for the final blow before his strength left his body.

Thanks to many rounds with the Society, Chase finally had Craig's arm bent behind his back and a knee to the backside to push him to the ground. "You want to keep going?"

"Let me up." Craig pleaded. "I'm an ass, Chase."

"Something we can finally agree on." Chase released his hold. "Here are my terms. You sell all your Falcon stock…to me."

"What? No way. Who do you think you are? Just because you're rich, you think you call all the shots? Well, you don't. I bought those stocks with my hard-earned money."

Chase slipped his phone from his pocket. "One call is all it takes. Decide. Stockbroker or police."

Sweat had broken out along Craig's hairline, his face beet red as he paced the floor. "How much?"

"For the stock?" Chase lifted a shoulder. "Whatever you paid for it."

"That's highway robbery!"

"Craig, you don't appear sorry for what you've done, so I'll make the choice for you. Police."

When he finished the call, he shoved Craig into a chair. "Stupid bastard. I'll still get those stocks and you're going to jail."

Danielle rushed into the room. "There's a police car outside, flashing lights and all." She looked to Craig and back to Chase. "Should I send them back?"

Chase nodded and turned to Craig. "Once the preliminary report is in on the car, I'm sure I'll have a case against you."

"You've got no proof," Craig growled. "You said so yourself."

"You're slipping, Craig." Chase held up his phone. "I do now." He stepped into he hallway to talk to the police.

"We'll take him down to the station and book him for attempted murder," one of the officers told him. "We're familiar with your case and will check on your car's status."

"Should be completed by the end of today," Chase told them.

"Those reports usually take three weeks, not three days." The other officer shook his head.

"Please, do me a favor, check." *It's done, trust me.*

"Will do." They entered the room and Chase heard them read Craig his rights.

Chase caught a glimpse of his reflection in the glass. The gauze bandage stood out and he decided to go to the same emergency room and find out if it could be removed. He stepped back as Craig was lead out of the room in handcuffs and shook his head. The plan was to get the shares and fire the guy. Too bad he'd made the wrong choice.

* * * *

"Oh, he gets me so mad at times!" Grace stared at her phone as it continued to ring. "Do not go to voicemail! Argh! It just did." She'd left Chase two messages already. He'd promised to call every hour but never did. "Well, truthfully, those were my rules, not his."

As soon as she hung up, her phone rang. "Hello?"

"Hey, baby."

"Don't 'hey, baby' me! Where have you been? I was worried sick."

"I'm walking out of the hospital with a much smaller bandage on my head. Got the all clear, and stitches come out next Tuesday."

Grace let out a breath. "You were at the doctor's? I didn't think you would go back to see him."

"Don't you love surprises?" Chase chuckled. "I have one more in store for you. Dinner is being delivered to your place in an hour. Meet me there?"

"Yes, I'm leaving now."

Relieved, yet mentally exhausted from the day, Grace stopped at her dad's office before leaving to check in on him. "You okay, Dad?"

Paul sat with his head in his hands like he'd done in her office. Grace never put her phone away and dialed June's number.

"Hi, Grace, need a sub for a flight?"

"No, June, nothing like that. Can you come to Falcon? Dad needs you."

"Is Paul okay?"

"He's fine, well, mentally we're both messed up, but it will help if he can talk to you."

"I'll be right there."

"I'll wait for you, June. We've locked the door for the day."

Grace slipped into a chair across from her dad. "We're not the perfect family, Dad."

"Never said we were, Dumpling." Paul lifted his head. "It has nothing to do with the family. I blame myself. I've been going over and over the events in our lives, especially Mark's, to see if I can come up with an answer. I thought I treated you kids equally and fairly."

"You did!" Grace got up and pulled her chair around to his side of the desk. She took his hand. "Each one of us had different needs and personalities and you catered to us individually. I never felt slighted or felt you owed me."

"That's good to hear." Paul patted the top of her hand. "Still…"

"Mark's made you feel guilty, Dad. Let it go or it will consume you."

"Do you remember when Sean died?"

What? "Yes, of course, I do."

"Even though you had nothing to do with his death, you blamed yourself. You felt you should've stopped him from leaving."

Oh. "You feel you should've known what Mark was doing and stopped him."

"Yes, Gracie," Paul whispered.

"It took me a long time to get over Sean and what happened, but I also refused to move on. You have someone to help you. And speaking of June…" Grace got up, grabbed her keys and headed for the front door.

June's car pulled up to the main entrance as Grace unlocked the door. She stepped outside and gave June a condensed version of the day. "Dad needs you, June. Don't let him wallow in self-pity as long as I did." Grace kissed the woman's cheek. "Thank you…in advance."

"Are you meeting Chase?" June patted Grace's face as she nodded. "You go, and I'll tend to Paul."

Grace waited until June was inside and walking down the hall before she relocked the door. Three cars were left in the parking lot, so she knew they'd be alone. The muggy air surrounded her like a cloak, yet it felt good. Grace took in a long breath of city air and let it out. *Time to start your life now, Grace Edison. Chase is waiting.*

A strange SUV was parked in her driveway and it took a minute to realize it was the rental. Chase sat in one of the wicker chairs, looking handsome as ever. Her heart flipped as she approached, reaching out to lightly touch his new skin-tone bandage. "Looks good." She teased.

Chase glanced at his watch. "Dinner should be here in fifteen minutes."

"I'll get the door." Grace heard a car motor as she pushed it open.

"Mr. Garrett?"

"Yes." Chase nodded. "This way." He held back the screen door for the young woman who carried a vase of two dozen pink roses.

"Oh!" Grace backed into the foyer to give her room. "Put them anywhere."

"Glass coffee table, please," Chase called from the porch.

Grace saw him hand her cash on her way out, but she wasn't done. The young woman handed Chase a silver bucket from the back of the van with two champagne bottles sticking out of it.

"That should do it. Thanks." Chase nodded.

Grace raced to get the door, and Chase stepped inside, kissing her as he passed by her.

"This is too much." Grace shook her head.

"You might not say that after I tell you what we can do with them later." Chase teased.

"If you're trying to take my mind off today, you're doing a good job." Grace slipped her arms around his waist. "Thank you." She paused. "I called June. She's with Dad."

"What about Tim? Does he know?"

"I don't think so, but it can wait a day. I doubt Mark went to see him."

Chase popped the cork on the bottle. "To us. It's been almost two weeks since I met you. You've changed me, Grace Edison, for the better. I love you."

Her heart melted as she took the flute of champagne from him. "I love you, too. Who knew when we first met we'd be standing here in love *and* having saved Falcon from ruin."

"Strange, right?" Chase lifted his brows over his glass as he sipped. "But, meant to be."

CHAPTER SEVENTEEN

Chase had talked to Mr. Smith on the drive to Grace's. He had congratulated Chase on a job well done. Questions about Craig and Mark swirled in his mind as they talked, but he knew Smith wouldn't give him a straight answer. One thing he did discover, Nash had begun his assignment as soon as he touched down in Miami. His first week was almost complete. *Good luck, buddy.*

Dinner had been delivered per his request from an expensive French restaurant, servers included. They'd followed instructions to the smallest detail. Chase didn't want dirty dishes messing up his last night with Grace for six weeks. One worker snuck away, sight unseen, to open Grace's bed and sprinkled red and white rose petals on the sheets. Another popped the second bottle of champagne and refilled the bucket with ice.

Chase had requested no scented candles, although many were lit throughout the house and out to the patio. He wanted to breath in Grace, fill himself up with her with no distractions. He fought down the melancholy that wanted to consume him. *You will see her again. She won't be mad…right.*

"Chase, this is lovely, but you don't look like you're enjoying it as much as I am."

"It's the people. Once they leave, I'll be fine." He didn't like the excuse since his house was filled with paid help. *Another lie to smooth over.* "You know I had two dogs back in Cleveland." He had no idea why he brought up the retrievers. *You want her to know something about your real life.*

"You couldn't bring them with you to Charlotte?" Grace gave him a look of sympathy.

"Sadly, no."

"That's a shame. What were their names and what kind of dog?" She smiled at him assuredly. "I hope they went to a good home."

"Belle and Bear were golden retrievers. Good friends took them. In fact, they were such great dogs, everyone wanted them."

"Do you think you could get them back one day? Buy a house?" Grace glanced around the patio. "No pets are allowed here. Otherwise, I'd say send for them."

The comment made him love her all the more. "They shed." He cocked his head.

"That's why vacuums were invented." Grace smiled over her glass. "This is really good champagne."

"Should I get the next bottle?"

"Please." Grace held up her glass when Chase returned. "I'm starting to like what I'm learning about you. You had two dogs, your mother remarried, and you have a sister in college."

"I did have a sister in college. Ella graduated earlier this month. It is still June?"

"Yes," Grace said with a laugh. "I know what you mean. It's been a long month."

Chase locked away the memory of her laugh, the way her eyes sparkled when she did and how absolutely happy she looked. Grace was relaxed, not on guard, but soon would change back to self-protection mode once he left. A twinge of guilt spread through him and he fought it down. *Make it the best night ever for both of you.*

"What does Ella want to do now that she graduated?" Grace asked.

"The usual stuff kids want to do, travel the world, become a model, anything but work." He winked.

"I could help with world travel, although Falcon would really have to expand if I wanted to offer her a free flight." Grace smiled. "How about New York City? I could fly her there to start a modeling career."

"She wishes."

"I remember you saying she could be one." Grace narrowed her eyes. "You don't want her to."

"I don't get a say, but if I did? No. It's a cutthroat industry."

"You're very interesting, Mr. Garrett. You seem to know about a lot of things."

Chase lifted a shoulder. "Stuff I hear from friends."

"Oh, we're back to friends. I never did meet the one you made plans with on Sunday."

"You will." Chase leaned forward and took her hand resting on the table. "That and more. What about you? Friends? I've gotten to know your family, but you haven't mentioned anyone else."

"I became a recluse after Sean died. My college friends moved, married, got jobs across the country. My best friend in high school lives in Florida. All my friends now are Falcon people, Halle being the best. They could tell when I was down, and they'd drag me to any bar having a special. You know, five-dollar margaritas and all the chips and salsa you can eat."

"Those are the kind of friends I like."

Grace smiled. "I'm friends with Jen, Tim's wife. After the third kid, we spent less time together. I can't imagine what it'll be like after Tim junior is born."

"Are they going with the name?" Chase mulled over Chase junior and decided he'd want his son to have his own name. *Son? We've only dated two weeks!*

"Yes, they are. Jen insisted."

"Do you know what I insist?"

"What?"

"We take our glasses and the bucket of champagne to your bedroom."

"To be continued?"

"Yes." Chase tucked the container under an arm and grabbed his glass. He'd peeked in the room before they came outside and gave it silent approval. Not too many rose petals, a few chunky candles lit, shades drawn.

"Oh!" Grace covered her mouth with a hand. "When did you have time to do this?"

"*I* didn't. It came with the service."

"Chase, you're spoiling me."

"You deserve to be, Grace. Don't let anyone ever tell you anything else."

"I have a surprise for *you*. Get comfortable and I'll be right back."

Comfort level was boxers for him and when he turned toward the bathroom, Grace came out in sheer white baby doll lingerie. He noticed the string bikini through the fabric and fought for control. "You look like an angel."

"Don't call me an angel tonight, Chase."

Grace was a breath away. The scent of magnolias filled his senses, and he wanted to freeze the moment. *I don't want to leave. I can't leave her.*

Her lips were upon his and Chase's mind became a blank slate. All he could think of was her, having her right now in this bed, then taking her home so he'd never be without her.

* * * *

"French toast!" Grace squealed. "The theme continues."

"They left me the ingredients so I could cook for you this morning." Chase flipped a piece of bread into the mixture.

"Mmm, smells good."

"You know what I'd like to do today?" Chase tossed the slice onto the griddle. "Swim in your wonderful private pool, just you and me."

"It will be filled with people now that you want it to yourself." Grace teased.

"We found a private spot, didn't we?" Chase raised his brows.

"You want to stay here, not go out for the day?"

"Here is fine. After all," Chase said and touched his head. "I'm still recovering."

"Do you think you'll have a scar?"

"Yeah, but I'm okay with it."

"Darcy will never stop teasing you about not being perfect anymore."

"Maybe it's a good thing. I don't have to be perfect. I don't need every hair in place and to trim my beard twice a day."

"Twice a day?"

"Once in the morning, once before bed." Chase smirked. "What can I say?" He plated the French toast and took it to the breakfast bar where he'd set the butter and syrup. "When does Darcy start work?"

"Monday." Grace slipped behind him and put her arms around his waist, placing her cheek on his back.

Grateful she couldn't see his face, Chase answered. "Thank you for helping her, Grace." *But I won't be there to see Darcy's first day on the job.*

After breakfast they watched a random house renovation show on TV, snuggling together and not really watching.

"Swim time," Grace announced.

"I have my suit in the car, give me a minute." Chase winced as he walked to the garage and out to his car. A hurriedly packed suitcase had been shoved in the trunk yesterday when he stopped by his place for a final visit. He had no plans to go back to his apartment once he boxed and donated everything but his clothes. Keeping Grace in the dark hurt the most when it came to the plan, but a necessary evil. "Yeah, a Smith evil."

As they strolled to the pool, children's voices could be heard. Chase looked at Grace. "I thought this was an adult only complex."

"It is. Sometimes on weekends, people have grandchildren visit. It's allowed." Grace poked him in the side. "We'll sit at the deep end."

A set of grandparents sat in the shallow end with two children under the age of five. They lifted their hands in recognition. "Hello, Grace. We're babysitting for the day and hoping to tire them out for a long afternoon nap."

Grace stopped at the edge of the pool. "Gloria and Jerry? This is Chase."

"Finally!" Jerry exclaimed. "It's about time someone snatched up this pretty little filly. Right, Gloria?" Jerry nudged his wife.

"Absolutely! But, I must say, my dear, it was worth the wait." Gloria lifted her sunglasses and stared at Chase.

"Good seeing you," Grace said and took Chase's hand, tugging him farther down the walkway and around the edge of the deep end, giggling. "We can't even see them from here."

"I hope those kids get tired soon. Not that I don't like children." Chase held up his hands. "I wanted today to be about us."

"That's sweet." Grace pulled two chaises close together.

They dozed in the sun for an hour and both looked at each other at the same time. "Is it quiet?" Chase asked.

"Yes," Grace whispered and started laughing. "Let's get in before anyone else comes."

Her arms were around his neck as they floated through the cool water. Chase ran his hands over her body again and again to memorize every part of her. They swam to the shallow end and raced back to their side of the pool, laughing and splashing when they arrived.

"I would like to take you out for a romantic dinner tonight," Chase said, kissing her cheek.

"I accept." Grace lashes fluttered. "I need time to get ready, and you'll want to get back to your apartment to change."

"I came prepared. I didn't want to spend a minute away from you." Chase kissed her lips, tasting chlorinated water mixed with her sweetness.

"We'll have to shower together then," Grace said between kisses.

"How could I refuse an offer like that?" Chase swam to the ladder and climbed out of the water, turning to assist Grace. He wrapped a towel around her and grabbed his things from the table.

Chase had left both phones in Grace's condo. She'd offered him the second bedroom as a place to get ready and he headed there to check for messages. The burner had a text from Smith. It said, *End it now.* Fire shot through his veins and he answered back, *After dinner!*

The phone sat silent in his hand as Chase waited for an answer. "Good. You got the message."

"Chase! Come on! The temperature is just right." Grace's voice called to him. She was all that mattered now. He'd completed his assignment, solved the mystery and wanted to focus on how to explain his departure.

* * * *

"I love the necklace," Grace said, turning toward him as they entered the condo after dinner.

Chase had wanted to spend more money on the heart-shaped necklace yet held back. Grace might become suspicious getting an expensive gift, although she'd never guess the platinum heart had handpicked quality diamonds set into place.

"I love the two diamonds hanging from the point. It represents us, right?"

"Yes, I'm glad I didn't have to say, 'Look! It's us.'" Chase chuckled, then grew serious. "I need to talk to you, Grace, and you're not going to like it."

"What is it?" Her brow wrinkled, and he longed to kiss away the confused look.

"I have to leave for a while."

"Oh! Is your mom sick? Sister, okay?"

"They're fine…it's…"

"You want to break up, don't you?" A look a terror crossed her face.

"No! It's just the opposite. I don't know how else to put it except to come out and say it. I won't be able to see you for six weeks and I don't want you to break up with me."

"Six weeks?" Grace raised her brows and tears filled her eyes.

Chase slipped an envelope from the inside pocket of his jacket and placed it on the island counter where they stood. "Can I ask you a favor? Don't open this for six weeks. But, please promise me you will. After you read it, make your decision if you still want to be with me or not."

Grace's jaw dropped, and Chase could tell she was processing the information. "I *will* be back for you, if you don't come to me."

"Then don't leave."

"I wish I could tell you more, why I have to leave. It's hard to ask you to trust me." Tears welled in his eyes. "Can you?"

"I want to."

Chase pulled her body so close to his they breathed the same air. "I love you. I don't want to leave you, Grace." He found her lips, grazing them lightly. She didn't return the kiss. "Come on, baby. Please?"

Grace stared into his eyes as if looking for the truth. Her hands wound around his back and into his hair. Her soft lips found his, and she gave him a kiss to remember. His heart beat against his chest and every nerve stood on edge. If she continued, he'd relent.

"Will it make you stay?" Grace asked, caressing his face.

"You know I want to." Chase took her by the arms and held her away from him so he could look at her one more time. "Walk me to the door?"

"No! If I do, then I'm agreeing to your idiotic terms."

"All right. I'll leave you here." Chase walked to the front door, opened it and forced himself to step onto the porch.

"Please!" Grace cried from the kitchen. "Don't leave me."

Chase winced at the familiar words, the ones she'd said to Sean long ago, as he walked toward his car. He couldn't look back. If he did, he'd never leave.

CHAPTER EIGHTEEN

Stunned, Grace stood in the kitchen, sobbing. She heard herself asking why too many times and snapped herself back to the reality of the situation. "You son of a bitch!" she screamed, flew into the great room, picked up the glass vase of two dozen roses and heaved it across the room.

Glass shattered everywhere. Water splattered the walls. Grace glanced around, looking for anything he had given her to destroy. Her hand came to rest on the heart necklace. She yanked it from her neck and threw it into a pile of the sad-looking roses lying on the floor.

"He was a player after all! What was I thinking? Good-looking, kind and caring? What a fool you are!" Grace walked to the kitchen island where Chase had set the letter. "Don't open this for six weeks." She mimicked. "But, please promise me you will."

Grace played with the envelope and held it up to the light. "I should open it now, that'll show him." She threw it back on the counter, jammed her hands on her hips, tears streaming down her cheeks. "Or I should forget him and get back to my old life. It was a pretty good one, right?"

After Grace pulled herself together and cleaned up the mess she'd made, she called her dad and said, "Tell me about him. You've been dying to for a week."

"I don't think now's the time, Gracie. You seem pretty upset."

"Upset? Try shocked and angry. Chase just left me. Oh, let me rephrase. He'll see me in six weeks or whenever he gets around to it."

"Let's try again when you feel better, Gracie. Remember the first time I tried to tell you about Chase, you stopped me. You were right to do so. He should be the one to tell you."

After Sam Young's visit, Paul had grown curious. The name Chase Young had stuck with him, and he'd given in and done an engine search. Grace had received a phone call while Paul still perused the internet. "I've got big news for you, Dumpling. You may or may not like it," he had told her.

"I'm listening."

"It's about Chase. I thought something was up when Sam Young showed up unannounced at Falcon. Chase is not who we think he is. I'm looking at a picture of him standing…"

"Let me stop you right there, Dad. I don't want to know. If Chase has something to tell me, he will."

"It's funny it didn't dawn on us sooner, Gracie. Think. I'm sure you'll come up with an answer without me having to tell you."

* * * *

The next morning, Grace's phone rang, startling her from a fitful sleep. She knocked it from the bedside table and scrambled to find it on the floor. Breathless, she answered, "Chase?"

"No, it's Tim."

"Oh."

"Don't sound so disappointed, baby sis."

"You don't sound great yourself." Grace sat up cross-legged on her bed. "Why are you calling so early on a Sunday?"

"I talked to Dad last night, Gracie, late into the night. I didn't get much sleep and decided to call."

"He told you about Chase?"

"What? No! He told me about our wonderful brother, Mark, and how he tried to help the family by sabotaging the company. And, he blames it on this other guy, Craig Hawk? What is he, five?"

"At times, I wonder if he ever grew up, Tim. He's had over-the-top ideas which should never see the light of day since he started working here."

"I heard you let him have it."

"I did, but it's your choice how you want to deal with him. I couldn't cut him off for good. He's family, but he'll never work at Falcon again."

"I agree with everything you said. My kids adore him, and I can't find it in my heart to be so ruthless. It will take time, but we can forgive him."

"It's been hardest on Dad." Grace let out a breath. "If we all agree, it will make things easier."

"Dad told me it was hard to fire Mark."

"He didn't. I did."

"Well, you know what he means." Tim paused. "Is something going on with Chase? Something I don't know about?"

"We're taking a break, Tim. Supposedly for six weeks."

"You feel like it's more than that, it's over before…"

"Can we change the subject again, Tim?"

"Sure, noticed how I picked up on our old saying?" He chuckled. "Jen's been overwhelmed here, and we never got to properly thank you for the giant baby basket which arrived unannounced at our doorstep. The girls loved it, too, and have been helping her put the baby stuff in the right drawers and closet. You are thoughtful, sis…and deserve better."

"Tim…!"

"Sorry, had to get it in. And…I'm saving the biggest thanks for last. I got your email last night. The money was more than I expected. Thank you from the bottom of my heart."

"You deserve it, Tim. I know Chase accused you of tampering with my computer."

"He told you?"

"No, I figured it out when he said he came to my office after hours and found you instead of me."

"We worked it out, Gracie. I like the guy. Maybe he's right about a break and will…"

"Stop. Go no further. You're welcome for the baby clothes and raise. You'll stop by the office tomorrow?"

"Yeah. Whatever you need, I'm here for you."

* * * *

The plain white envelope had taken over her existence for a month and half. Grace had left the letter where Chase had placed it and talked to it every day while she got ready for work, ate at the counter or poured a glass of wine. Her favorite line was, "Stop staring at me!" Then, she'd flip it over to the other plain side.

On Saturday, exactly six weeks to the day, Grace let her overwhelming curiosity take over. She made coffee, showered and dressed, forcing herself to stick to a daily routine. When she settled in at the counter, her fingers walked toward the envelope, and she slid it in her direction. "The answer's in here, and you want to know. You *deserve* to know."

To her surprise, only an address had been written in the middle of the paper. "What?" She recognized the city, not far from town. "You'd have to have a six-figure income to live there, no, make it seven."

Her laptop sat next to her. Grace had planned to read work emails while she had breakfast. Now, her mission changed. She flipped up the top, opened a window and typed in a name. "Chase Young."

Scanning the websites, she picked a society article written in the local paper. "Why didn't I connect the name with the man. Sam Young didn't hide the fact Chase was his son. Oh." She tapped her forehead. "He wasn't in on the game. And what game were you playing, Mr. Young?"

Grace read countless articles on the young billionaire, Chase Young, a different girl on his arm in every picture. She then found his company, C. Y. Airlines, and was stumped. "Craig Hawk worked for you and slashed your brake line?" Grace wrinkled her brow and slapped the counter. "Didn't I read Hawk cut a deal and will do two years of jail time? You let him off easy, Chase." She paused, trying to think back to the news report. "And, I don't recall reading your name in the article."

As hard as she tried, she couldn't come up with a connection between Chase, Craig and Falcon.

Her eyes grew wide as understanding began to take shape. "Oh! Now I get it. Chase must have gone there to check on his company, and Craig got nervous. Chase picked up on the fact, did a little digging, and found my brother's number on Craig's desk. But! Craig wouldn't have known Chase was one of our pilots." Tears burned the back of her eyes. "He thought his boss was on to him and wanted to stop Chase from interfering." She looked at the ceiling. "Oh, Chase, he tried to kill *you*, not one of our pilots! How did you keep it together without giving anything away? You could've told me the truth. I would've been there for you."

Without being present, Chase had finally cracked her resolve and stubbornness of forgiving him. She wanted to let him tell his side of the story. He'd put his life on the line for Falcon, and they never knew…until now.

* * * *

Grace sat at the end of the long driveway, looking at a magnificent modern two-story home which fit perfectly into its surrounding landscape. "This can't be the right address."

Although, she knew it was.

Shocked by Chase's announcement, the pain still resonated through her body whenever she thought of the night he said goodbye. He'd left her six long, excruciating weeks ago. She pictured the scene in the kitchen where she'd cried for hours.

Grace shook her head, trying to bring herself to the present, except both conversations she had with her Dad kept creeping into her mind. "Yes, Dad. Maybe somewhere deep inside me, I knew he was lying. Chase was in my life for all of two weeks, promised we'd be together long term, then left. I wanted to wipe his memory from my mind. He could have been hiding from the law or a mastermind thief or spy or maybe an ordinary guy trying to survive out there like the rest of us and I'd still love him." She lifted one side of her mouth. "Instead?" Grace reached for the envelope on the passenger's seat. "I thought this would reveal everything I needed to know about him, but there's only an address of a billionaire's house printed in the middle of the paper."

She thought back to her morning's search on the laptop, and it gave her mixed emotions. "You came here to give him a chance. Let him speak. Let's finish what we started."

Grace stepped on the gas pedal and traveled up the long drive. Unsure where to park, she noticed other vehicles parked in extra spots by a four-car garage at the side of the house. She took a deep breath and exited the car. "Now what?" She glanced around, taking in the beauty which surrounded her.

A box on the garage caught her eye, and she approached, hoping it was some type of security system and doorbell. Not wanting to go to the front of the house, she pressed a button, hoping it worked.

"Hello?" a female voice answered.

"Hello, my name is Grace Edison. Is Chase home?"

"Grace?" The voice sounded excited.

"Yes."

"I'll be right there."

A door to the far side of the garage opened and a lovely Latina woman, who appeared to be in her early fifties, stepped out. "Grace," she said, extending her hand in greeting. "I am Chase's house manager, Renata."

Grace took her hand, feeling the warmth of the greeting. "He's been a nervous nut all day, wondering if you'd come."

Two golden retrievers bounded from the door and jumped around Grace, but never on her.

"Belle and Bear." Renata smiled. "I forgot to shut the kitchen door tight. The little rascals don't like to be left alone."

"Belle and Bear?" Grace gasped. "May I pet them?"

Renata said something in Spanish, and the dogs sat at attention. "They are friendly. Go on."

Tears filled her eyes as she spoke to and petted each one. "They are beautiful." Grace sniffed.

"Chase will have my head if I don't get you to the bunker." Renata threw her hand in the air. "Follow me."

"The bunker?"

"The boys named it. Don't ask me why." Renata chuckled.

"The boys?"

"I am sorry. I keep forgetting you don't know them. It's been quite a summer." Renata shook her head.

"Tell me about it." Grace had to agree. "Should I prepare myself?"

Renata stopped on the stone trail and looked at her. "For?"

"More than one man in the bunker? I saw cars in the lot, unless they belong to Chase."

Renata laughed. "Oh, yes, there will be more than one man. But, I am sure Chase has them under control."

"I'm sure he does." Grace's heart beat faster as they came closer to a ranch-style home. "This is the bunker? It looks like a vacation home."

"Yes, and I'm sorry in advance if it is not as clean as I would like it to be. Some parts are off-limits to my staff."

Grace turned toward the sound of a waterfall. "Do I hear…?"

"Yes, a waterfall. It's coming from the pool. My grandchildren love it, especially the slide."

"They come here often?"

"Oh, yes, my family was here in June. Chase built a home for me on the grounds, and I hate to leave it."

"Where does your family live, may I ask?"

"Miami."

Something rang a bell when she heard Miami, but Grace was overwhelmed by the sights and sounds on the property. "This is so beautiful. I bet it's hard to leave."

"Come." Renata lifted the door knocker and tapped three times, waited and did two more. She stepped away and placed Grace in front of her.

The door swung open, and Chase stood on the other side dressed casually in shorts, a t-shirt and sandals. "You came!"

"I did." Grace looked down at the stone walkway, then felt her body being pulled into his arms.

"Oh, baby, I am so sorry I had to leave you. I promise I will answer all your questions if we have to stay up all night."

Grace peered over his shoulder at five pairs of eyes staring at her. "Uh, Chase?"

"Them?" he whispered in her ear. "Ignore them." He kissed her hello. She threw caution to the wind and kissed him back with equal passion as cheers erupted in the room. She leaned back and lifted the front of his hair to check the scar.

"Still there, but the doctor said it should fade in time." Chase placed his arm around her waist and turned her toward the men seated in recliners and on a rounded leather sectional. "Grace? I'd like you to meet my friends, the best guys you'll ever meet. We met in college and have been…"

Someone in the room cleared their throat and Chase shot a look his way as if sending daggers.

"It's nice to meet you all," Grace said, scanning the room to make eye contact with each man.

Chase guided her into the room for introductions. Nash rose from his seat. "Grace, good to see you again."

"I'm not surprised to see you, Nash." Grace smiled.

The couple made the rounds, talking to Finn, Beau, Kade and Gabe, all handsome, fit men. Although they all were welcoming, Grace felt something was off. She felt the tension of unspoken secrets. *Of course, they would. They don't know me.* She looked to Chase. He still had a secret. Would she ever find out what it was?

* * * *

That night, sitting cross-legged on his bed and wearing one of his white dress shirts, Grace peppered Chase with questions until he held up his hands.

"One at a time, please." His body shook as he laughed, and she couldn't take her eyes off his handsome face. "Let me ask you one."

"Okay." Grace wondered what he could ask, since he had all the answers.

"Do you think Halle would accept Craig's position at my airline?"

"You're going to steal her away from us?" Grace shook her head then smiled. "I don't know. You'd have to run it by her. It's a great opportunity. I wouldn't stop her from taking it."

"It's only fair. You get Darcy. I get Halle."

"We're swapping best friends?" Grace giggled.

"Yeah." Chase looked over his shoulder. "Wouldn't you rather be in my lap pool? It's right outside my bedroom."

"You promised you'd answer everything." Grace jutted out her lower lip. "We're not even halfway. From what you've told me, a friend suggested you needed to check out Falcon, something was amiss and could affect you and maybe your business. Instead of asking direct questions, you applied for the pilot's job which I *know* we never placed."

"Do you think anyone would have answered direct questions?" Chase chuckled, ignoring the comment about how he got the job. "I decided to go undercover. It worked out pretty well."

"Especially the part when you totaled the car." Grace rolled her eyes. "Seriously, Chase, you could have been in the hospital with broken bones, internal injuries or worse. Now I have all the facts, it's beyond comprehension someone you trusted to run C.Y. could betray you in such a backhanded way."

"Neither can I." Chase dropped his head and folded his hands. "You're right about the good outcome. I'm sorry I put you through it … again."

"You scared me, Chase. But I've tried to let go of the past and not compare. When you walked out the door, I said, 'Don't leave me', but I was only talking to you, no one else."

Chase lifted his head and locked eyes with her. "I know."

Grace covered her heart with her hand. "Good. I have one more question about your friend. He warned you about Falcon, but we have nothing to do with you or your airline. Why did you believe him? Please explain."

"I thought it strange, too, but I guess he wasn't quite sure what was going on and wanted me to do some detective work. He thought it could affect C.Y. If

I found nothing, no harm done. Besides, I met you. I should thank him."

Grace gave him what she hoped was a sultry smile. "Last question. Why did I have to wait for six weeks until I saw you again?"

Chase got up from the oversized upholstered chair and strolled to the bed. "So you'd miss me." He bent down, arms on either side of her, planting a sweet kiss on her mouth.

Grace fell into the mattress, taking him with her. He'd answered her questions, they'd saved Falcon, and they were together. What more could she want?

His lips leisurely moved from her mouth to her ear, then neck and Grace gave up questioning him for the night.

He can't still be hiding something, could he?

The End

PREVIEW
NASH
The Secret Billionaire Society
BOOK 2

PROLOGUE

"Mr. Nash Gill?" the voice said over the speakers.

"Present and accounted for Mr. Smith!" I raised my hand like I remembered Chase had when he was given the first assignment. He was the leader of our group, although he hated to admit it, and I followed his lead. "Yes, sir. I'm ready for duty. Cue the music."

I expected the *Mission Impossible* theme song to start up but only heard the breathing of my buddies around me.

"Be serious, Nash," Chase's voice came from behind me.

I could be serious as the next guy, but what was life without a little fun? My motto had been live fast and furious until I met these five guys in college. I passed up a football scholarship to attend Harvard and thank goodness I did. Not every guy made it to the NFL, and I'd been smart enough to realize it. My dream had always been the same since middle school, own a gym. Back then, I oddly thought I could work out for free and hang with the customers. The older I got, I realized I needed business skills, networking and marketing experience. Where else better to learn the ropes than Harvard?

My roommate was a great guy from the New York City area, Beau Miller, and we'd quickly made friends with Chase Young and Finn Larsson who lived down the hall. Finn was from California, a rich guy's son, who wanted out from under his daddy's shadow, and Chase was driven to become something even back then. We added Gabe and Kade to the group sophomore year, and we'd been tight ever since.

Chase had been the first to see my potential, encouraging me to follow my dream of opening a fitness center in Miami. I owned a chain of them now, Gill's Gym, in Florida and one in Charlotte, North Carolina, Chase's hometown.

In fact, I was in Charlotte now. I sat in the bunker, as we called it, a place Chase had built on his property in North Carolina. Actually, it was a glorified man cave, the outer room filled with manly toys and the inner sanctum, where only the six were allowed, looked like an interrogation room with a one-way mirror and two rows of seats. We'd entered the room as a unit when Mr. Smith came to call.

Who in the hell was Mr. Smith? We had no idea. I thought back to our thirtieth birthday bash, all celebrated on the same day, an annual tradition since we graduated from college and went our separate ways. We'd come from all parts of the country to attend Harvard and on our birthday, no one could keep us apart. Thirty was big, or as I'd heard it called, Dirty Thirty … didn't know why, but I liked it. Turning the big three-o got us thinking. What had we done with our lives?

We'd formed the Secret Billionaire Society as a joke our junior year at Harvard, swearing we'd all be one by the time we reached thirty. To our surprise, it happened sooner rather than later, thanks to Chase's investment skills and Finn's ties to people with money and connections. The three of us were the first to agree to the made-up club. I dragged Beau into the society kicking and screaming. He insisted he could do it without help. But once he heard the pledge, we'd help each other no matter the circumstances, he was in.

Kade and Gabe were the creative types and didn't care about money in college. Then, they came to their senses. To follow their dreams, they needed cash or investors and jumped in feet first. Or headfirst? Whatever.

I learned to slow down but never gave up having a good time. I also despised being looked at as a jock because I worked out and liked it. Two lines of Chinese script tattoos ran down the inside of one bicep which made some think I was vain, all about the body and the look. Maybe a day's worth of stubble didn't help either. I shrugged it off long ago. No one, except these guys and my former girlfriend, knew I was a big softie inside.

On the fateful thirtieth birthday night, we drank, sang and reminisced until one in the morning. All went well until someone had gotten melancholy and asked if this was all there was to life—partying, drinking and making money. I stood, beer in hand, and gave quite the speech about the qualities of those three exact things. Someone threw wads of alcohol-soaked napkins in my direction as I broke into song. After the fight had calmed, we stared at each other for the longest time. It became the lightbulb moment and when Mr. Smith was born. The man behind the mirror. We'd never met him. We didn't know what he looked like. Yet, we'd agreed to put our lives in his hands and trust him.

We only knew his name—Mr. Smith. He was now in charge of us. He'd receive all we owned if we did not follow through with the assignments. That became our motivation, get our money back from him. If one failed, we all did. We thought Smith had selfless goals when we hired him at four a.m. that night, spouting how much he liked our talk of doing something for the greater good. He promised to fit the assignments into our lives. Maybe he didn't have selfless goals after demanding our assets go into a trust. He could end up with all our money, but the Society agreed we wouldn't quit the project. We'd succeed no matter what.

During the birthday night, I found the *Mission Impossible* theme song and kept playing it during key moments. I thought it added suspense, but someone, no make that two guys, had to wrestle my cell away from me and threw it into another room. Couldn't a guy have a little fun? Sure, this was serious, we might have to start over again financially if we didn't complete our missions. Yet at five in the morning, no one seemed to care about the money. For a birthday bash, we'd gotten way too serious on how to save the world or let us get real … one person. Money be damned. I had liked the partying mood we'd established earlier in the night and wished to get back to it.

Before ending the call with Mr. Smith, the six of us had been instructed to put together dossiers. A special courier would retrieve the drives on a set day and deliver them to Smith. Once he had the memory stick in hand, he'd know everything about us. The only thing we asked was to give each of us a separate assignment. He could set the parameters, make the rules.

After Smith received and read our bios, another courier would deliver the next set of instructions. Mr. Smith took no chances and didn't want us to use our cell phones, email, texts, or any technical means of communication to contact him. The first message we received had been to build a soundproof room where we could meet, and the bunker was born.

Once built, we'd get our assignment and instructions in the room plus a burner phone, like Chase had, whenever we needed to speak to the man. Smith had already tweaked the rules for my mission after speaking with Chase. The rest of us could keep our real phones, besides the burner, a lesson learned from the first assignment.

"Mr. Gill?" The voice called to me again.

What happens next? Find out in
Nash The Secret Billionaire Society Book 2
Always free on Kindle Unlimited

The $ecret Billionaire $ociety (Contemporary Romantic Suspense)

Chase (Book 1)

Nash (Book 2)

Finn (Book 3)

Beau (Book 4)

Gabe (Book 5)

Kade (Book 6)

The Elusive Mr. Smith (Book 7)

Smith's Revenge (Book 8)

BEFORE YOU GO

THANK YOU FOR READING

Did you enjoy this book?
I invite you to leave a review at your favorite book site, such as
Goodreads, BookBub and Amazon.

DID YOU KNOW THAT LEAVING A REVIEW...

Helps other readers find books they may enjoy.
Gives you a chance to let your voice be heard.
Gives authors recognition for their hard work.
Doesn't have to be long. A sentence or two about why you liked the book will do.

OTHER BOOKS BY NANCY PENNICK

Waiting for Dusk Series (Young Adult)

Waiting for Dusk (Book 1)

Call of The Canyon (Book 2)

Stealing Time (Book 3)

Taking Chances (Short Story)

Broken Dreams (Prequel)

Twenty Nine Series (Young Adult)

29

29 Squared

29 Degrees

29 Forever

The Clan MacLaren Series
(Historical Romance)

My Highlander Husband (Book 1)

Donnach's Daughter (Book 2)

The Heart of the Emerald (Book 3)

Now and Forever (Book 4)

MacLaren Strong (Book 5)

Homecoming (Book 6)

ABOUT THE AUTHOR

Nancy Pennick, author of young adult and romance books, has been writing nonstop since retiring from teaching. Starting off as a young adult author, she has enjoyed diving into other genres. In other words, she likes to write whatever comes to mind! Born and raised in Northeast Ohio, she resides in Mentor, OH. Nancy is married and has one son.